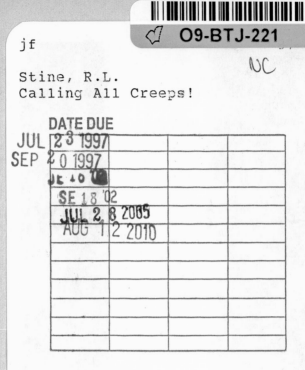

**Look for more Goosebumps books
by R.L. Stine:
(see back of book for a complete listing)**

#15 The Werewolf of Fever Swamp
#16 One Day at HorrorLand
#17 Why I'm Afraid of Bees
#18 Monster Blood II
#19 Deep Trouble
#20 The Scarecrow Walks at Midnight
#21 Go Eat Worms!
#22 Ghost Beach
#23 Return of the Mummy
#24 Phantom of the Auditorium
#25 Attack of the Mutant
#26 My Hairiest Adventure
#27 A Night in Terror Tower
#28 The Cuckoo Clock of Doom
#29 Monster Blood III
#30 It Came From Beneath the Sink!
#31 Night of the Living Dummy II
#32 The Barking Ghost
#33 The Horror at Camp Jellyjam
#34 Revenge of the Lawn Gnomes
#35 A Shocker on Shock Street
#36 The Haunted Mask II
#37 The Headless Ghost
#38 The Abominable Snowman of Pasadena
#39 How I Got My Shrunken Head
#40 Night of the Living Dummy III
#41 Bad Hare Day
#42 Egg Monsters From Mars
#43 The Beast From the East
#44 Say Cheese and Die — Again!
#45 Ghost Camp
#46 How to Kill a Monster
#47 Legend of the Lost Legend
#48 Attack of the Jack-o'-lanterns
#49 Vampire Breath

Goosebumps®

CALLING ALL CREEPS

R.L. STINE

AN
APPLE
PAPERBACK

SCHOLASTIC INC.
New York Toronto London Auckland Sydney

A PARACHUTE PRESS BOOK

ISBN 0-590-56887-6

12 11 10 9 8 7 6 5 4 3 2 1   6 7 8 9/9 0 1/0

Printed in the U.S.A.   40

First Scholastic printing, December 1996

CALLING ALL CREEPS

1

At a little after eight o'clock at night, I tiptoed from my bedroom and crept as silently as I could down the stairs. Three steps from the bottom, I tripped over a stack of laundry — and fell head-first the rest of the way.

I landed hard on my elbows and knees, but I didn't make a sound. I'm used to falling. I do it all the time.

I jumped quickly to my feet and peeked into the front hallway. Had Mom and Dad heard me?

They had the TV on in the den. They were watching the Weather Channel. They can watch the Weather Channel for *hours.*

What's so interesting about the weather?

I could hear the woman on TV talking about the wind chill in Nova Scotia. I pulled on my blue down parka and made my way silently to the front door.

A few seconds later, I was outside, jogging

along the sidewalk. I kept in the shadows, ducked my head low — and headed for school.

Don't get the wrong idea about me. I don't usually sneak out of the house at night. I'm not a problem child or anything. In fact, my parents are always telling me to be braver, to be more adventurous.

I never go out without telling my parents where I'm going. But tonight was a special night. Tonight I had a special mission.

The mission was spelled r-e-v-e-n-g-e.

I slipped as I reached the corner and had to grab a lamppost to keep myself from falling. Most of the snow from the weekend had melted. But there were still slick patches of ice on the sidewalk.

I hadn't bothered to zip up my parka. The wind blew it behind me as I jogged across the street and past the small houses on the next block. The air felt cold against my warm cheeks, and wet, as if it might snow again.

Hey — enough about the weather!

Ricky Beamer — that's me — had more important things on his mind tonight. Tonight I planned to do a little spying. And then a little nasty mischief.

A few minutes later, I made my way across the deserted playground next to the school. Harding Middle School. That's what the sign beside the bare flagpole read. Except that someone had spray-painted over all the first letters. So the sign actually read: ARDING IDDLE CHOOL.

We have a lot of school pride here at Harding.

Actually, most kids like the school. It's really new and everything is modern and clean.

I'd like our school too — if the kids would give me a break. If they'd all get out of my face and stop calling me Ricky Rat and Sicky Ricky, I'd be a real happy guy.

Maybe you think I sound a little bitter.

Maybe you're right!

But all the kids think I'm a nerd. They make fun of me every chance they get.

I stared at the school building. It's kind of low and flat and curves around like a snake. The elementary school is at one end, and the middle school is at the other. I'm in sixth grade, so my classroom is right in the middle.

A spotlight shone down on the bare flagpole in front of the building. Behind it, most of the classrooms were dark. I saw lighted windows at the eighth-grade end — and that's where I headed.

A car rumbled past slowly. Its headlights washed over the front of the building. I ducked behind a tall evergreen bush. I didn't want to be seen.

In my rush to hide, I stumbled into the bush. A clump of cold, wet snow plopped onto my head. With a shiver, I shook my wavy black hair to toss it off.

3

When the car had passed, I crept up to the lighted classroom window. My sneakers made squishing sounds in the soft ground. I glanced down. I had stepped into a deep, muddy rut.

Ignoring the mud, I leaned against the low window ledge and pressed my face to the glass. Were the lights on because the night janitor was cleaning in there? Or was Tasha McClain hard at work?

Tasha McClain. Just saying her name made my teeth itch!

The windowpane was steamed up. I squinted through the glass. Yes! Tasha sat at the desk against the wall. She leaned over her computer, typing away. Her long, curly red hair fell over the keyboard as she typed with two fingers.

Ms. Richards, the newspaper advisor, stood beside her, one hand on the back of Tasha's chair. Ms. Richards is young and *very* pretty. She had her blond hair pulled back in a ponytail. In her baggy gray sweatshirt and faded jeans, she looked more like a student than a teacher.

Ms. Richards was nice to me last September when I signed up for the school newspaper staff. But she's been pretty mean lately. I think Tasha turned her against me.

Tasha is an eighth-grader, so she thinks she's hot stuff. Sixth-graders are *nothing* at Harding. Believe me. We're *nothing*. Maybe even less.

I knew Tasha and Ms. Richards would be

working late on the *Harding Herald* tonight. Because tomorrow is Tuesday, the day the paper comes out.

Ms. Richards leaned over Tasha and pointed to something on the computer monitor. I squinted harder to see the screen. I could see a headline with a photo beneath it.

Tasha was laying out the *Herald* front page.

Once she had the front page finished, she would save it on a disk. Then Ms. Richards would take the disk to the laser printer in the main office and print out two hundred copies.

Ms. Richards turned suddenly to the window. I dropped to the ground.

Had she seen me?

I waited a few seconds, then pulled myself up. Tasha was typing away. She stopped every few seconds to click the mouse and move things around on the screen.

Ms. Richards walked out of the room.

I shivered. The wind swirled, fluttering my parka hood. I hadn't brushed all the snow from my hair. Cold water dripped down the back of my neck. I heard a dog howling sadly in the distance.

Please get up! I silently urged Tasha.

Please leave the room too — so I can play my little joke.

On the street behind me, another car rumbled past. I pressed myself against the dark wall, trying to make myself invisible.

When I moved back to the window, the classroom stood empty. Tasha had also left the room.

"Yesss!" I cheered softly.

My heart pounded with excitement. I raised both hands to the windowsill. I struggled to push up the window so that I could climb inside.

I knew I had to be quick. Tasha probably had gone down the hall to the juice machine. I had only a few seconds to get in the room — do my damage — and get out of there.

I pushed and strained. The window didn't budge.

At first I thought it might be frozen shut. But finally, on the fourth try, it started to slide up. I pushed with all my strength — and opened the window just enough to squeeze through.

My wet sneakers slid on the linoleum floor. I was leaving a trail of muddy footprints, but I didn't care.

I crept across the room and hunched down in front of the computer. My hand shook as I grabbed the mouse and moved to the bottom of the newspaper page.

I heard voices. Tasha and Ms. Richards talking out in the hall.

Taking a deep breath, I frantically studied the page.

Then I typed a few words — in tiny, tiny type — at the bottom of the front page. Giggling softly to myself, I wrote:

Calling All Creeps. Calling All Creeps. If you're a real Creep, call Tasha at 555-6709 after midnight.

Why did I add this little message to the front page of my school newspaper?

Why did I sneak in at night and risk getting caught?

Why did I desperately *need* to get revenge against Tasha?

Well . . . it's sort of a long story. . . .

2

A few days ago, a new girl started at our school. Her name is Iris Candler. She walked into my class and stood awkwardly at the front of the room, waiting for Ms. Williamson to assign her a seat.

I was busy trying to do the math homework assignment before the bell rang. Somehow I forgot all about it the night before.

I took a few seconds from my furious scribbling to check out the new girl. Kind of cute, I thought. She had a round face with big blue eyes and short blond hair parted in the middle. She wore long, red plastic earrings that jangled when she moved her head.

Ms. Williamson gave Iris a seat near the back. Then she asked me to show Iris around the school during the day. You know. Point out where the lunchroom is and all the bathrooms and everything.

I nearly cried out in surprise. Why did Ms. Williamson pick me? I guess it was because Iris just happened to be sitting right next to me.

I heard a couple of kids laugh. And I heard someone mutter, "Sicky Ricky."

Kids in my class are always on my case. I hoped that Iris didn't hear them.

I admit it. I wanted to impress her. I liked having someone new to talk to, someone who didn't know that everyone thought I was a loser.

At lunchtime I walked Iris downstairs to the lunchroom. I told her about how new the school was. And how when we moved in for the first time, hot water came out of all the cold water faucets, and cold water came out of the hot.

She thought that was pretty funny. I liked the way her earrings jangled when she laughed.

She asked me if I was on any sports teams.

"Not yet," I answered.

Not in a million years! I thought.

Whenever guys are choosing up teams on the playground, the captains always fight over who gets me. It's always:

"*You* take him!"

"No fair! *You* have to take him!"

"No. *You* take him! We had him last time!"

I'm not exactly a super jock.

"This is the lunchroom," I told Iris, leading the way through the door. I instantly felt really dumb. I mean, what *else* could it be? The band room?

As soon as I entered, I saw my four enemies at their usual table in the middle of the room. I call them my four enemies because . . . they're my four enemies!

Their names are Jared, David, Brenda, and Wart. Wart's name is really Richard Wartman. But everyone calls him Wart — even the teachers.

These four seventh-graders are always making fun of me. When they're not making fun of me, they're trying to *injure* me!

I don't know what their problem is. I never did anything to them. I guess they pick on me because I'm easy to pick on.

I grabbed two food trays and guided Iris to the food counter. "This is hot food over here," I explained. "No one ever eats the hot food unless it's pizza or hamburgers."

Iris flashed me a nice smile. "Just like at my old school," she said.

"Be sure to stay away from the macaroni," I warned. "No one ever eats the macaroni. We think they serve the same macaroni all year. See that crust on top? Whoever heard of macaroni with a crust?"

Iris laughed. I brushed back my hair. I wondered if she liked me.

We both picked up sandwiches and bags of

potato chips. I put a bowl of red and green Jell-O and a bottle of kiwi-strawberry drink on my tray. "The cashier is over here," I told Iris.

I showed Iris how you hand your food ticket to the cashier and get it punched. I was feeling pretty good. I think Iris was impressed by all my helpful instructions.

I spotted a couple of seats at a table near the window. I motioned to them with my head. Then I started through the crowded, noisy room, holding my tray high in both hands.

Of course I didn't see Wart stick his foot out.

I tripped over it. Fell forward. And my whole tray went flying.

I hit the floor in time to look up and see the red and green Jell-O bound across a table and onto a girl's lap. The rest of my food slid over the floor.

Kids laughed and cheered and clapped.

"There goes Ricky!" someone exclaimed. "Ricky Rat! Ricky Rat!"

Wart and his three pals started chanting: "Sicky Ricky . . . Sicky Ricky!"

I glanced up and saw Iris laughing too.

I just wanted to disappear.

My face suddenly felt burning hot. I knew I was blushing.

What am I going to do? I thought, lying there on my stomach. *I really can't take this any longer.*

What can I do?

3

After school I made my way to the eighth-grade classrooms at the end of the building. The school newspaper office is in Ms. Richards's room.

Ms. Richards sat at her desk, grading papers. As I stepped into the doorway, she glanced up and frowned. Then she returned to her work.

I saw Tasha typing furiously at the computer in the corner. Her lips moved as she wrote. Her forehead furrowed in heavy concentration.

I walked over to the assistant editor, an eighth-grader named Melly. Melly has short, straight brown hair and wears glasses with brown frames that match her hair. She was leaning over a long news story, running her finger down the page as she read.

"Hi, Melly," I said.

She glanced up and frowned too. "Ricky — you made me lose my place."

"Sorry," I said. "Any stories for me today?"

You probably wonder why I signed up to be a

reporter on the *Harding Herald*. It's not that I'm a great writer or anything.

Every kid at Harding needs twenty activity points a year. That means you have to try out for sports or join clubs or other after-school activities.

No way I was going to try out for a sport. So I signed up for the newspaper. I thought it would be easy.

That's because I hadn't met Tasha yet.

Tasha treats all sixth-graders like bugs. She makes a disgusted face when a sixth-grader walks into the room. Then she tries to step on us.

She gives all the good story assignments to eighth-graders. Do you know the first story she asked me to write? She asked me to count the dirt patches in the playground and write about why grass didn't grow there.

I knew she was just trying to get me out of the office. But I wrote the story anyway. It's hard to write a good story about dirt patches. But I did a really good job. My story was five pages long!

She never printed it in the paper.

When I asked her why, she said, "Who cares about dirt patches?"

My next assignment was to interview the night janitor about the differences between working days and nights.

That one didn't get into the paper, either.

I wanted to quit. But I really needed the activity points. If I didn't earn twenty activity points, I couldn't graduate from sixth grade. I'd have to go to summer school. Really.

So I kept coming to the *Harding Herald* office two or three afternoons a week after school, asking Tasha for more news stories to write.

"Anything for me?" I asked Melly.

She shrugged. "I don't know. Ask Tasha."

I moved over to Tasha's desk. Her face reflected the blue monitor as she typed away. "Any stories for me?" I asked her.

She kept typing. She didn't glance up. "Wait till I'm finished," she snarled.

I backed away. I turned and saw Ms. Richards walk out of the room. Some kids were talking by the table near the window, so I crossed over to them.

David and Wart — two of my enemies — were arguing about something. They're both sports reporters for the paper. They write about all the Harding games. The rest of the time they hang around the office, making trouble.

David is tall and blond. Wart is short and lumpy and red-faced. He looks a little like a wart!

I saw some cookies and cans of soda on the table. I tried to walk around David and Wart to get to the drinks. But Wart stepped in front of me.

He and David both grinned. "How was your lunch, Ricky?" Wart asked.

They laughed and slapped each other a high five.

I glared at Wart. I wanted to wipe the grin off his face. "Why did you trip me?" I could feel my face growing hot.

"I didn't," he lied.

David laughed.

"You did too!" I insisted. "You stuck out your foot —"

"No way," he said. "I didn't touch you."

"You tripped over a crack in the floor," David chimed in. "Or maybe it was an air pocket."

They both laughed.

They're so lame.

I grabbed a can of Pepsi off the table, popped it open, and started to walk away.

"Hey, wait —" Wart held me by the shoulder.

I spun around. "What's your problem?"

"That's the can I wanted," he said.

"Too bad. Get your own," I told him.

"No. I want that one." He swiped at the can.

I swung my hand out of his reach.

Lost my grip. And the can went flying across the room.

It sprayed Pepsi as it flew. Then landed in the middle of Tasha's keyboard.

She let out a squeal. Jumped up. Knocked her chair over.

I quickly grabbed up a handful of paper napkins from the table and darted across the room.

"Don't worry. I'll clean it up!" I told Tasha.

The keyboard was soaked. I frantically started to mop the keys.

"No — Ricky — *stop*!" Tasha shrieked.

Too late.

I stared in horror at what I had done.

4

"Aaaaiiiiii!" Tasha opened her mouth in an angry scream. She tugged at her red hair with both hands.

"You creep! Ricky, you creep!" she cried.

She shouldn't call people names. But she had good reason to be angry at me.

I had erased the whole front page.

The screen glowed at us. Bright blue. Solid blue.

No words. No pictures.

"Uh . . . sorry," I murmured.

"Maybe I can get it back," Tasha told Melly. "Maybe there is a way to find it and pull it back up."

Tasha shoved me out of the way, picked up her chair, and sat down. "Oh!" She let out another cry when she realized she had sat in a puddle of soda.

Staring at the solid blue screen, she began typing furiously.

I could see that the keys were still wet and

17

sticky. She kept making mistakes. Backing up. Typing again. Typing. Typing. Muttering under her breath the whole time.

No use. No good.

The front page refused to come back.

Finally, she gave up with a loud groan. She tossed her hair in the air with both hands. And turned to me with a growl.

"You creep!" she cried. "All that work! All that work — lost!"

I swallowed hard. "Tasha, it was an accident," I muttered. "Really. It was just an accident."

"You little creep!" Tasha shrieked. Melly stood beside her, glaring at me angrily, shaking her head.

"Wart pushed me!" I cried. I turned to the table. Wart and David had vanished from the room.

"You're off the paper!" Tasha screamed. "Get out, Ricky. You're out of here!"

"Huh?" My heart stopped for a second. "No, Tasha — wait!" I pleaded.

"Get out! Get out!" She made shooing motions with both hands. The way you shoo away a dog. "You're off the paper! I mean it!"

"But — but — but —" I sputtered like an outboard motor. "But I need the activity points! Please give me a second chance! *Please!*" I begged.

"Out!" Tasha insisted.

Melly tsk-tsked and shook her head.

"You're so *unfair*!" I wailed.

I know, I know. I sounded like a baby. But, give me a break. It really *was* unfair.

I turned and slunk to the door. And guess who was standing there. Guess who had watched the whole ugly scene.

You're right.

Iris.

Her first day of school. And she already knew what a loser I was.

"What are *you* doing here?" I asked glumly.

"They said I needed an after-school activity. So I thought I'd try the newspaper," Iris replied. She followed me down the empty hall. "But I don't think I want to join the newspaper. That red-haired girl is really mean."

"Tell me about it," I muttered, rolling my eyes.

"She shouldn't have called you a creep," Iris continued. "It was just an accident. She's horrible! She should give you another chance."

Maybe Iris and I *will* become good friends, I thought.

I pulled my blue parka from my locker. Then Iris and I made our way out of the building.

The afternoon sun was already dropping behind the houses and bare trees. It gets dark so early here in the winter. Patches of snow on the lawns and sidewalk gleamed dully as we walked toward the street.

"Which way is your house?" I asked, shifting my backpack over my parka.

Iris pointed.

"Mine too," I said. We started walking together. I didn't really feel like talking. I was still totally upset about getting kicked off the newspaper.

But I felt glad that Iris was on my side.

We crossed the street and made our way up the next block. A tall hedge stretched along the entire block, broken only by driveways.

Some kids had marked off the street for a street hockey game. They were skating back and forth, leaning on their sticks, cheering and shouting.

"Do you skate?" Iris asked.

"A little," I told her. "My Rollerblades are kind of broken. The brakes came loose and —"

"I always take off the brakes," she said. "It's a lot more fun without the brakes — don't you think?"

I started to answer. But a sound from behind the tall hedge made me stop.

Was someone whispering?

Did I hear someone giggling?

Iris and I kept walking. She was telling me something about how kids skated in the town she moved from. I didn't really listen.

I kept hearing footsteps. Whispers. Scraping sounds. From the other side of the hedge.

Finally, I raised a finger to my lips. "Iris —
shhh," I whispered.

Her blue eyes widened in surprise. "Ricky —
what's the matter?"

"I think we're being followed," I told her.

5

"I don't hear anything," Iris whispered. She narrowed her eyes at me.

We both listened.

Silence. Except for the cheers of the street hockey players behind us down the block.

We started walking.

I heard a giggle. Some whispers.

I turned into the next driveway and darted behind the hedge.

"Who's there?" Iris called. She came running up behind me. Her eyes searched the hedge, then the front yard.

"No one here," I said.

She laughed, "Ricky, why do you look so worried? You probably heard a bird or something."

"Yeah. A bird," I repeated. I led the way around the hedge to the sidewalk. I didn't want Iris to think I was crazy. But I knew I'd heard something.

We walked past a few more houses. Then I

heard a whispered chant from behind the hedge: "Sicky Ricky . . . Sicky Ricky . . ."

"Did you hear that?" I asked Iris.

She shook her head. I heard the distant hum of a plane, high overhead. "Do you mean that plane?" she asked.

"No," I replied. "I heard a voice."

A soft giggle floated out from the hedge.

I ran to check it out. Nearly slipped on a slick patch of ice.

I grabbed the hedge to catch my balance. No one back there. An empty front yard.

Straightening my backpack, I hurried to Iris on the sidewalk.

"Ricky, you're a little weird," she said. She laughed. But I could tell she was starting to wonder about me. Starting to think maybe I was too weird to be her friend.

"I heard someone back there. Really," I insisted. "They must be hiding in the hedge or —"

"AAAAAIIIIIII!" I heard a scream of attack!

The hedge shook.

I staggered backwards toward the street.

And four figures came leaping out of the hedge. Four kids shrieking and cheering.

My four enemies!

I saw Iris's face twist in surprise. And then Wart grabbed me. David grabbed me too. Brenda and Jared joined them.

They pushed me one way. Then pulled me back.

Laughing and shouting, they spun me around.
Then David tackled me to the ground.

They swarmed around me. Pushed me down. Held me in the cold, wet mud.

"Let go of me!" I shrieked.

I tried to kick and thrash and squirm free. But the four of them held me firmly.

"Let go of me!" I wailed. "What are you going to do?"

6

"Let him go!" I heard Iris cry.

"Okay," Wart replied. "No problem." The big chubby wart had been sitting on my chest. He climbed to his feet.

I took a deep breath.

The other three let go of me and took a step back.

I sat up, rubbing mud off my parka sleeve. I glanced at Iris. She stood near the curb, hands balled into fists, her eyes wide with alarm.

With a groan, I started to stand up.

But Wart and Jared shoved me back down. "Not so fast," Jared said. Jared is short and skinny, but he's real mean.

"What do you want?" I demanded.

Wart leaned over me. "Why did you tell Tasha that the soda can accident was my fault?" he asked.

"Because it *was* your fault," I shot back. I pulled a dead brown leaf from my hair.

"But why did you tell Tasha?" Wart asked nastily.

"Because he's a wimp," David chimed in.

"Because he was scared," Brenda said.

"Because you're a snitch," Wart accused.

"But it *was* your fault!" I cried. I tried to climb up, but they pushed me down again.

Iris let out a short cry, then covered her mouth with both hands. I could see she was really scared. "Don't worry," I called to her. "They're not really going to hurt me."

I turned to Wart. "Right?"

All four of them laughed.

"What should we do to Ricky Rat?" Brenda said.

"Hurt him," David replied.

They laughed again.

"No. Let's make him sing," Wart said, grinning at me.

"Oh, no!" I groaned. "Not again!"

They think it's a riot to make me sing songs to them. They force me to sing all the time. It's because I have a terrible voice, and I can't carry a tune. "Please —" I begged.

"Yes. Sing a song — for your new friend," Brenda said, motioning to Iris.

"No. No way!" I insisted.

David and Jared bent down and grabbed my shoulders. They started to push me deeper into the mud. "Sing a song," Jared ordered.

"Sing *The Star-Spangled Banner*," Wart said.

The others cheered and clapped. "Yes! *The Star-Spangled Banner*! That's the best!"

"Noooo," I groaned. "Not again. Please, guys! Please! I don't know the words. Really. Don't make me sing that song again!"

I begged and pleaded. Iris begged and pleaded.

But the four of them stood over me, staring me down, not letting me up from the mud.

What choice did I have? I knew only one way to get them to leave. So, sitting there on the cold, muddy ground, I started to sing.

"Oh, say can you see . . . ?"

They burst into loud laughter. They hooted and howled. They shoved each other and slapped each other high fives. They practically fell down in the mud themselves, they were laughing so hard.

". . . and the hooooome of the brave."

Somehow I made it through the whole song. Of course, I forgot most of the words. And of course my voice cracked at the high parts.

And of course I'd never been so embarrassed in all my life.

Iris must think I'm the biggest jerk on the planet, I told myself. She must think I'm a total loser.

I wanted to sink into the mud like a worm and never come back up.

I took off. I just started to run.

I didn't glance back. Not at my four enemies. Not at Iris.

Especially not at Iris. I didn't want to see her laughing at me too.

Or feeling sorry for me.

I ran all the way home without slowing down. Then I burst into the house. Slammed the door behind me. And ran up to my room.

This is all Tasha's fault, I decided.

First Tasha kicked me off the newspaper staff — because of an accident. Then Tasha told Wart that I had blamed him.

So Wart and his pals had no choice. They *had* to chase after me and embarrass me in front of Iris.

All Tasha's fault . . . all Tasha's fault . . .

I was still thinking about her as I struggled to fall asleep that night. Still thinking about how I'd pay Tasha back some day.

It took hours and hours to fall asleep.

The phone beside my bed rang and woke me up Saturday morning. Sleepily, I grabbed up the receiver.

Guess who was on the other end?

Tasha.

Yes. A surprise call from Tasha.

A call that would change my life.

7

"Huh?" I managed to choke out, still half asleep. I cleared my throat.

"I need your help," Tasha said.

"Huh?" I sat straight up in bed. Tasha needed *my* help? Was I *totally* asleep? Was I dreaming this?

"I need you to cover a story for me," Tasha continued. "For the newspaper. I've tried everyone else I know. They couldn't do it. You are the last person I wanted to call. But you're my only hope."

"Huh?" I replied.

"Ricky — is that all you can say?" Tasha demanded shrilly. "Did I wake you up or something?"

"Huh? Uh . . . no." I cleared my throat again. I shook my head, trying to force myself to be alert.

Tasha needed my help?

"I need you to come to school and cover the

Midwinter Car Wash," Tasha said. "I need a story and photos. Right away."

"Huh?" I replied. Why couldn't I stop saying that? I guess I was in shock or something. "A car wash in winter?"

Tasha sighed. "You don't know about the school car wash? Didn't you see all the signs? Don't you read the newspaper?"

"Oh. Right. I just forgot," I lied. I peeked out the window. Golden sunshine. Nice day for a car wash.

"Great! I'll come right to school, Tasha," I told her. "Thanks for giving me another chance."

"I didn't want to call you," she said coldly. "But most of my reporters went on a field trip. And the others are working at the car wash. If my dog could take pictures, I would have used him."

"Thanks a lot!" I cried.

I know. I know. She was trying to insult me.

But she was also giving me a chance. Maybe I wouldn't have to take summer school after all.

I pulled on a pair of faded jeans and a sweat-shirt. Gulped down a fast breakfast — some kind of pink, blue, and green cereal and a glass of orange juice. Then I ran all the way to school.

It was a warm day. On the radio, they said it would snow tonight and tomorrow. But it felt too warm to snow.

As I crossed the street to the school, I saw kids setting up the car wash on the playground. A white banner, fluttering in the morning breeze, proclaimed: HARDING CAR WASH — $5.

Kids were stretching long hoses from the back of the school building. Several buckets were set on a long wooden table, along with sponges and a stack of white towels. A blue Pontiac and a mini-van were already in line to be washed.

I hurried into the building and down the hall to the newspaper room. I found Tasha all alone in the classroom. She leaned over her computer, typing away.

She frowned when she saw me run in. "I'd do the story myself," she said. "But I have to finish up the features page. I've never been this desperate."

Nice greeting, huh?

"I'll do a good job. I promise," I said.

She crossed the room and picked up a camera from Ms. Richards's desk. "Here. Take this, Ricky." She handed it to me. "And be careful with it. It's my dad's Pentax. It's really expensive, and it's his favorite camera."

I held the camera carefully in both hands and examined it. I raised it to my eye. "Say *cheese*," I said.

Tasha didn't smile. "I'm warning you, Ricky," she said sternly. "Don't let anything happen to that camera. Take four or five different shots of kids washing cars. Then bring it right back to me."

31

"No problem," I told her.

"I want the story to be six or eight paragraphs," she continued. "You'll have to write it today and get it to me by tomorrow at the latest. Ms. Richards and I are going to finish laying out the paper and print it Monday night."

"No problem," I repeated.

"I'm saving a column on page two," Tasha said. "So promise me you won't mess up this time."

"I promise," I said.

Then I turned and hurried out to the playground.

I can do this, I told myself. I can handle it.

I can turn my life around this morning. Everything will be great after I do this assignment.

That's what I told myself.

But as soon as I arrived at the car wash, my life was ruined.

8

Squinting into the bright morning sun, I jogged across the playground. My sneakers slipped in the wet grass. I carried the camera carefully in front of me in both hands.

As I came closer, I shielded my eyes from the sun with one hand. I recognized the blue Pontiac. It belonged to Wart's parents. Kids with hoses surrounded it, spraying it on all sides.

Raising the camera, I ran toward the car. "Hold it right there!" I called. "Let me take a picture for the *Herald*!"

The first spray of water shocked me.

I felt something hit the front of my sweatshirt. Something cold.

I let out a startled cry.

The next two sprays hit me in the face and the chest — and sent me sprawling backwards.

"Hey — !" I managed to shout. "Stop it! Are you *crazy*?"

I tried scrambling out of the way. But now there were *four* hoses trained on me.

"Ohhhh." The water was freezing cold!

Ducking out of the way, I recognized the four grinning faces aiming the hoses. Brenda, Wart, David, and Jared.

Who else?

Sputtering, I turned and tried to run out of range. Cold water sprayed down on me like a shower. Another hose caught me in the back.

"Stop it! Hey — stop it, you guys!" I cried.

And then I remembered the camera.

Ducking my head from another hard blast of water, I raised the camera.

Drenched. Totally drenched.

"Aaaaaiiiiii!" An angry scream tore from my throat.

Staring in horror at the dripping wet camera, I lost it. For the first time in my life, I totally lost it.

I strapped the camera around my neck. Then I spun around and hurtled toward my four attackers.

My last chance! I told myself.

My last chance on the newspaper — and they're *ruining* it!

Howling and giggling, the four seventh-graders tried to blast me back with their hoses. But I lowered my head and came at them.

Sputtering, shaking off water, I leaped on

Wart. I tackled him around the waist and dragged him to the ground.

He cut his laugh short with a startled gasp.

I grabbed the hose from his hand. Pulled open the door to his parents' car. And sent a spray of water into the car.

"Hey — noooooo!" Wart wailed.

Water from David's hose shot against my back. Water sprayed the air like a fountain. At the next car, I heard kids laughing and shouting in surprise.

I drenched the backseat and then the front.

When I saw Brenda, David, and Jared drop their hoses, I dropped mine too. And started to run.

They all chased after me.

I didn't get far.

The grass was so slippery and wet. I ran a few steps — and then my sneakers slid out from under me.

I went down hard.

Fell facedown into the grass.

On top of the camera.

9

"Does this mean I'm off the paper?" I asked meekly.

Tasha scowled and turned the camera over in her hands. "The lens is cracked," she murmured, shaking her head. "The whole camera is soaked and bent." Her voice trembled. "It – it's wrecked."

"It really wasn't my fault," I said softly.

She angrily blew a strand of red hair off her forehead. "You'll pay for it!" she cried. "You'll pay for the camera, Ricky. If you don't, my father will *sue* you!"

"But, Tasha —" I pleaded. "You know it wasn't my fault!"

"Go away," she snapped. "Just go away. Nothing is ever your fault — right?"

"Well . . . it wasn't," I insisted. "If you'd listen to me, Tasha —"

"You're just bad news, Ricky," she said, scowling at me again. She examined the broken camera one more time, then dropped it onto a desk.

"You don't take anything seriously," she accused. "You think everything is a goof."

"But, Tasha —" I started to plead.

"Go away," she said. "That was your last chance. You didn't deserve it. You're just a creep. Why do you think all the kids call you Ricky Rat? Because that's what you are — a little rodent!"

Those words really stung.

I felt a stab of pain in my chest. I struggled to breathe.

I spun around so that Tasha couldn't see how upset I was. And I hurried out of the room and out of the school.

As I ran across the playground, I heard kids at the car wash singing and laughing. They were soaping up cars, spraying them clean, having a great time.

As I passed by, I heard some kids start to chant, "Sicky Ricky, Sicky Ricky." And I heard some other kids laugh.

I turned my head away and kept running. I knew that by Monday, Tasha would have told everyone about how I ruined her father's camera.

The story would be all over school. Everyone would know how Ricky Rat had messed up again.

Running home with Tasha's words still in my ears, I felt more angry with each step. I wanted to scream. I wanted to *explode*!

That's when I decided to pay Tasha back.

That's when I decided to play a mean joke.

Creep . . . creep . . . creep . . .

The word repeated and repeated in my mind.

Ricky, you're just a creep. Just a little rodent.

You'll pay, Ricky. If you don't, my father will SUE you!

Rodent. Rodent. Rodent.

She had no right to call me that. It wasn't fair.

I had been so hurt, so angry. But by the time I reached home, I was smiling. I knew what I wanted to do. I knew how I was going to take my revenge.

I had my plan all worked out in my mind.

It couldn't fail. It couldn't.

So, here I am.

Monday night. I sneaked into the classroom where Tasha and Ms. Richards were working.

I gleefully typed my little message on the bottom of the front page of the newspaper.

I knew I had to hurry. Tasha and Ms. Richards would return any second.

I listened tensely for any sound, for any sign that they were near.

I had never been so nervous in all my life. But I also had a smile on my face.

Ricky, they all think you're a loser. But you're a genius! I congratulated myself.

Only you could have dreamed up such a wonderful, nasty revenge.

Glancing up at the doorway every two seconds, I finished typing in my message for Harding Middle School newspaper readers:

Calling All Creeps. Calling All Creeps. If you're a real Creep, call Tasha at 555-6709 after midnight.

I read it over. It made me smile again.

I felt like jumping up and down and laughing out loud.

But I knew I couldn't make a sound.

I stood up. Turned to the window. Started to make my escape.

Halfway to the window, I heard Tasha cough and step into the room.

I was caught.

10

I froze.

So close, I thought. *So close.* The window stood only five steps away. Five steps — and I would have been out of there.

But the five steps seemed as far as five miles now!

I shut my eyes and waited for Tasha to cry out.

Instead, I heard Ms. Richards's voice from out in the hall. "Tasha — would you come here for a moment?"

I opened my eyes in time to see Tasha disappear back out the door.

Had she seen me? No. No way. She would have screamed.

Whewwwwww! I let out a long sigh — and dove out the window.

I landed on my elbows and knees. Scrambled frantically to my feet. And started running.

I didn't even bother to close the window. Too risky, I decided.

For the third time in four days, I ran all the way home.

On Friday and Saturday I ran home a disgrace, a loser, a *creep*.

Tonight I ran home a winner. A champion! A genius!

I let myself silently into the house. I could hear voices from the TV in the den. Mom and Dad were still watching the Weather Channel.

I listened for a moment in the front hallway, catching my breath. Bad storms in the Pacific Northwest . . . flood warnings . . .

A few weeks ago, I tried to get Mom and Dad to switch channels to MTV. But they hated MTV because it never gave the weather.

I felt so happy, so excited. I wanted to rush into the den and tell them about my great joke.

But, of course, I couldn't do that.

Instead, I made my way silently up to my room and closed the door.

Who could I call? I *had* to call someone. I had to share my little secret with someone. But who?

Iris.

Yes. Iris. She would appreciate it. Iris would understand.

My heart pounding, I reached for my phone. It took me a while to remember Iris's last name. I had only heard it once. Chandler? Candle? Candler. Yes. Iris Candler.

I got the phone number from information and

called her. The phone rang once. Twice. Iris picked it up after the third ring.

We both said hello. She sounded surprised to hear from me.

"Guess where I went tonight?" I asked her. But I didn't wait for her to guess. I blurted out the whole story. It all just burst out of me. I don't think I took a breath!

"Is that great or what?" I demanded when I had told her every detail. I laughed. "The paper comes out tomorrow," I said. "Tasha won't be sleeping much tomorrow night. She'll be getting calls all night from every kid in school!"

I waited for Iris to laugh. But I heard only a long silence on her end of the line.

"Don't you think it's funny?" I asked finally.

"Kind of," she replied. "But I have a bad feeling about it, Ricky. A very bad feeling."

"Iris, it's just a joke," I told her. "What could go wrong?"

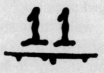

11

When I arrived at school the next morning, guess who I saw first.

You're right. Tasha.

She turned her nose up as if she smelled rotten fish. Then she hurried past me without saying a word.

I didn't care. I thought about my little surprise for Tasha on the bottom of the *Herald*'s front page. I knew it would keep me smiling all day.

Believe me, I needed something to smile about.

As I turned the corner to go to my locker, Josh and Greg, two kids from my class, deliberately bumped into me. "Ricky, stop bumping into me," Josh said.

Greg bumped me again. Then he pushed me into Josh.

"Hey — give me a break! I *said* stop bumping into me!" Josh cried.

"Get a life," I muttered. I dodged away from them.

They walked off laughing, bumping each other from one side of the hall to the other.

Funny guys, huh? About as funny as a broken arm.

I pulled open my locker and started unloading books from my backpack.

"Hey, Ricky — want to wash my dad's car?" a kid named Tony shouted from across the hall.

I had my head in my locker. I didn't look around.

I heard kids laughing at Tony's hilarious joke.

"Hey, Ricky — want to wash something?" Tony called. "Wash your face!"

What a joker.

Everyone laughed again.

I slammed my locker door and walked past them without saying a word. This is all Tasha's fault, I told myself. But I'm going to have the last laugh tonight.

I turned the corner and headed to class. I saw Brenda and Wart at the water fountain against the wall. I tried to run past them. But I wasn't fast enough.

Brenda pressed her hand over the fountain — and shot a spray of cold water onto the front of my shirt.

"Have a squirt — Squirt!" Wart called.

Big laughter, up and down the hall.

"My dad is *suing* you for wrecking his car!"

Wart called. "He's suing your family for every penny they've got!"

"Tell him to get in line," I muttered under my breath.

"Ricky Rat! Ricky Rat!" someone chanted.

Welcome to "Pick on Ricky Day" at Harding Middle School.

Unfortunately, *every* day is "Pick on Ricky Day."

But today I didn't care. Today I knew I'd end up a winner.

Today the joke was on Tasha. The student newspaper would be handed out this afternoon. And Tasha would be up all night, answering phone calls.

Sweet, sweet revenge was mine.

That night I had to go out for dinner with my parents and my cousins who live across town. Mom and Dad didn't bring me home until nine thirty, and I had about two hours of homework to do.

So I didn't tuck myself into bed until nearly twelve — very late for a school night.

I just started to drift off to sleep when the phone beside my bed rang.

I squinted at my clock radio — two minutes until twelve.

"Now who would call this late?" I asked myself.

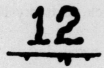

12

I fumbled for the phone in the dark. Knocked it off the bed table. It clattered loudly onto the floor.

I dove out of bed and grabbed the receiver. Then I hunched on my knees, listening for Mom and Dad. Did they hear the phone ring? I'm not allowed to get calls after ten o'clock.

I cleared my throat and raised the phone to my ear. "Hello?"

"Ricky — it's me. Iris."

I glanced at my clock radio again. "Iris? It's midnight. How come you're calling so late?" I asked. "Are you okay?"

"My father was on the phone practically the whole night. Ricky — did you see the school paper?" she demanded in an urgent whisper.

"Huh? No," I replied, climbing onto the edge of my bed. "When they started to pass out the newspapers, I got called to the library. The librarian wanted to ask me about a bunch of books

I lost. When I came back to the room, all the papers were gone."

"So you didn't see the paper?" Iris asked shrilly.

"No," I repeated. "I didn't get my copy. Is it great? Can you read the message at the bottom okay?"

"Well . . ." Iris hesitated.

"Is it great?" I asked excitedly.

"Not exactly," Iris replied softly. "Actually, Ricky, you're in . . . major trouble."

"I'm what?" I squeezed the phone to my ear. She was talking so softly, I could barely hear her. "Iris . . . I'm *what*?"

"In major trouble," she repeated.

A chill swept down my back. "Major trouble? But — why, Iris? What do you m-mean?" I sputtered.

"The message —" she started.

Then she stopped. Silence on the other end.

"Iris — I can't hear you!" I said. "Iris — ?"

"Uh-oh," she murmured. "I've got to get off. My dad is screaming at me."

"But, Iris —" I insisted. "Why am I in trouble? You've *got* to tell me!"

"*I'm getting off!*" I heard her call to her father. "*It was only a short call, Dad. I know it's midnight!*"

"Iris, please — tell me. Tell me before you hang up!" I begged.

"Got to go. Bye," she said. I heard a click. The line went dead.

I slammed the receiver down angrily. What was her problem? Why couldn't she tell me why I was in trouble?

I slid the phone back in place beside the clock radio and climbed into bed. I punched my pillow a few times, puffing it up. Then I pulled the blankets up to my chin.

I shut my eyes and tried to calm down enough to fall asleep.

The phone rang again.

I sat straight up with a startled gasp. This time I managed to pick up the phone without knocking it to the floor.

"Iris, thanks for calling me back," I whispered.

"I saw your message in the school newspaper," a voice whispered.

"Iris — ?" I swallowed hard. I knew it wasn't Iris.

"I saw your message," the voice whispered. "I am calling as you instructed."

"Huh? You're calling *me*?" I cried.

"Yes. I'm following your instructions," came the whispered reply.

"Hey — who *is* this?" I demanded.

"I'm a Creep."

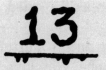

13

I slammed down the phone.

Then I settled back into my bed. I puffed up my pillows again, and pulled the blanket over my shoulders.

The wind howled outside my bedroom window. Shadows cast by the street lamp in front of our house danced over my wall.

My brain was spinning.

Who *was* that?

I couldn't be sure, but it sounded like a boy. Why did he call *me*? The message I put in the newspaper gave *Tasha's* phone number.

I didn't have long to think about it. The phone rang again.

I grabbed up the receiver before the first ring ended. My eyes shot to the bedroom door. If Mom or Dad heard me getting these calls, I'd *really* be in major trouble!

"Hello? Who is it?" I demanded.

"Hi. I'm a Creep." A different voice. A boy. Speaking softly.

"Huh?" I gasped.

"I'm a Creep. I called as soon as I saw your orders."

"Give me a break!" I cried. I slammed down the phone.

"What is going on?" I muttered out loud. I sat staring at the phone. Watching it in the dim light. Waiting.

Was it going to ring again?

"Ricky — !" a voice boomed.

I jumped a mile.

The ceiling light clicked on. Dad stood in the doorway in his blue-and-white striped pajamas. He scratched his cheek. "Ricky — what are all those calls about?" he demanded.

I shrugged. "Calls?"

He narrowed his eyes at me suspiciously. "I heard the phone ring three times," he growled.

"Oh. You mean *those* calls!" I tried to sound innocent. But I knew I didn't stand a chance.

"You know you're not allowed to get calls after ten," Dad said sharply. He yawned. "It is after midnight. Now *who* is calling so late?"

"It's some kind of a joke," I told him. "You know. Kids from school."

He brushed his sandy hair off his forehead. "I don't think it's funny," he said.

I lowered my head. "I know. But it isn't my fault —"

He raised a hand to silence me. "Tell your friends to stop," he said. "I mean it. If they keep calling so late, I'll have to take your phone away."

"I'll tell them," I promised.

I'd tell them to stop, I thought, *if I knew who they were!*

Dad yawned again. He has the loudest yawn in the world. It sounds more like a roar.

When he finished yawning, he clicked off the light and disappeared back to his room.

As soon as he left, the phone rang again.

"Please —" I started.

"I'm a Creep," a whispered voice told me. A girl this time. "I saw your message. I'm ready. Ready to plant. Ready to rule. When will the Creeps meet?"

"Huh? Meet?" I didn't wait for an answer. I hung up the phone.

Staring at the phone, I felt totally confused.

Why am *I* getting all these calls? I wondered.

Is there some kind of a mix-up?

And why are the calls so strange? Why did that girl say she's ready to plant? Ready to rule?

What is going on?

The phone rang again . . .

14

The next morning, I dragged myself to school. The phone hadn't stopped ringing until two in the morning. That's when I took it off the hook. I spent the rest of the night twisting and turning, thinking about all the weird calls.

I didn't fall asleep until seven. Which is the time my alarm goes off to wake me up!

At breakfast, my head nearly dropped into my corn flakes. I just wanted to go back to bed. But Mom and Dad didn't feel sorry for me at all.

They were furious. The ringing phone had kept them awake too.

"You tell those kids not to call again," Mom warned. "Or else I'll go in to your school and tell them myself!"

"No — please!" I begged. "I'll tell them. I'll tell them this morning! They won't call again. I promise!"

Can you think of anything more embarrassing

than having your mom come to school, barge into your classroom, and lecture the kids in your class?

They already make fun of me every day and call me "Sicky Ricky." Can you *imagine* what they would call me if my mom came to school and yelled at them all?

Whoa!

Just thinking about it gave me icy chills.

It took all my strength to pull myself to school and slump through the crowded hall to my locker.

"There you are!" Iris cried.

I saw her waiting across from my locker. She wore a loose plaid shirt over navy blue corduroy pants. Her long plastic earrings jangled softly.

She had been leaning against the tile wall. Now she pushed through a group of girls to get to me. "Here, Ricky. Take a look."

She handed me the latest copy of the *Harding Herald*. I grabbed it eagerly and lowered my eyes to the bottom of the front page.

Yes. There it was. In tiny type across the whole bottom margin. My message.

Except it had been changed a little.

I moved my lips, reading it softly to myself:

"Calling All Creeps. Calling All Creeps. If you're a real Creep, call Ricky after midnight." Then it gave my phone number.

My phone number. Not Tasha's.

My name and number.

I let out a low moan and weakly handed the paper back to Iris.

She shook her head and tsk-tsked. "You look terrible. Did you get any sleep at all?" she asked.

"No," I murmured.

I grabbed the newspaper back and read it again. "How did this happen?" I cried.

Tasha's grinning face flashed into my mind.

"Tasha!" I screamed her name. And then I took off, pushing my way through groups of kids, hurtling over someone's backpack.

I ran down the long, curving hall to the eighth-grade classrooms. And burst into Tasha's room just as the early bell rang.

My eyes frantically swept the room. I spotted her near the front, handing a notebook to another girl.

"Tasha —" I called, running up to her. I waved the newspaper in her face. "I — I —" I sputtered breathlessly.

She tossed back her red curls and laughed. "I caught your little joke just in time," she said. "Did you get any calls last night, Ricky?"

"A few," I muttered angrily.

The whole class burst out laughing at me. Even the teacher.

All morning, I had the feeling that everyone was watching me. Laughing at me.

Maybe I imagined it. Maybe I didn't.

I kept thinking about the calls I'd received the night before. I knew they were all from kids at school. But why were they saying such strange things?

I saw your instructions . . .

I'm ready to plant. Ready to rule.

When will the Creeps meet?

At lunch, I carried my tray toward the back corner of the lunchroom. I didn't feel like eating with anyone. I didn't feel like hearing more jokes, more kids laughing at me.

I had to walk past the table where my four seventh-grade enemies always sit.

Uh-oh, I thought. Wart and David were squirting their milk cartons at each other. Brenda laughed so hard, chocolate milk ran out of her nose.

They see me. I'm going to get a milk shower, I realized. Too late to go the other way.

To my shock, I passed right by the table without getting splashed or hit by anything. Wart didn't call out any nasty jokes. David and Jared didn't try to trip me.

What's going on? I wondered as I hurried to the far corner of the room. I know they saw me.

Why didn't they chant "Sicky Ricky" and toss their drink cartons at me the way they always do? They let me pass by as if they didn't know me.

I slid my tray across the back table. No one

ever sits in that corner. It's next to the furnace duct. Hot air blows out over the table while you eat.

I had picked up a sandwich of some kind of lunchmeat and a bowl of tomato soup. I tilted my chair back against the wall and sat chewing on the sandwich, watching the other kids.

Waiting. Waiting for someone to come over and make a joke about how my tomato soup looked like clotted blood. Or make a joke about all the calls I got after midnight.

Waiting for kids to start chanting "Sicky Ricky." Or for Wart or one of my other pals at his table to start throwing food at me.

But no.

No one paid any attention to me. I leaned back and ate my lunch in peace.

I finished the soup and half the sandwich. I had picked up a bowl of chocolate pudding for dessert. But the crust was too thick to force my spoon through.

I gathered up my tray and stood up to leave.

And someone hit me in the forehead with a wadded-up piece of paper.

"Hey — !" I called out angrily. But secretly I felt glad. I mean, I just didn't feel normal going a whole lunch hour without anyone getting on my case.

Rubbing my forehead, I glanced down at the

paper. And realized it had writing on it. A note. Someone had passed me a note.

I unfolded it and quickly read the scribbled words:

When will the Creeps meet?

15

I glanced around the room, trying to see who tossed the note to me. But no one seemed to be looking at me. Wart and his three friends were pushing in their chairs, carrying their trays to the tray deposit window.

Did one of them throw it? I wondered.

I read the note again, folded it up, and shoved it into my jeans pocket. Then I carried my tray to the window and hurried out of the lunch room.

I bumped into Iris in the hall. "What's up?" she asked.

I shrugged. "More Creeps," I told her. "They seem to be following me." I sighed. "I guess I asked for it."

"I told you I had a bad feeling about that joke of yours," Iris replied. "No way Tasha was going to let you get away with it."

"Don't rub it in," I murmured unhappily. "If kids start calling me again tonight, my parents will go totally ballistic. I'll lose my phone for sure."

"Maybe you should take it off the hook when you go to bed," Iris suggested.

Smart. Iris is very smart, I realized. I'm not sure I would have thought of that.

I led the way upstairs. Lockers were banging all around us. Kids were shoving in coats, pulling out books and notebooks, jamming stuff into their backpacks. It was almost time for the bell to ring.

Iris stopped at her locker and turned to me. Her cheeks suddenly had pink circles on them. "Would you do me a favor?" she asked.

"Sure," I told her.

Was she blushing? What was she going to ask?

"It's so hard being the new girl in school," she said. "I thought I'd try to make something really special for the school bake sale on Saturday. You know. Try to impress everyone with my school spirit. Rah rah!" She shot up both hands like a cheerleader.

I laughed and waited for her to continue.

"Well . . ." she hesitated. "Would you come with me after school tomorrow to help me buy supplies? Flour and sugar and stuff? We could go —"

"Of course!" I interrupted.

I felt so excited, I almost blurted out, "No girl ever asked me to go *anywhere* before!"

But somehow I managed to stay cool enough not to tell her that.

59

"I'll meet you behind the playground after school tomorrow," I said. "We can shop for whatever you need, and I'll help you carry it all home."

Big man, huh?

She thanked me, and I jogged down the hall to my locker. I actually felt like skipping — or flying! Iris likes me, I decided. A girl in my school *likes* me.

You probably think this is no big deal. But it was a very big deal to me.

It changed my whole mood. It made me forget about all the trouble I'd been having. It made me forget I was *me*!

What a great day! I told myself. What an *awesome* day!

My happy mood lasted until I opened my locker.

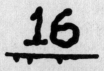

16

Humming to myself, I slipped open the locker door. I squatted down and started to pull some notebooks from the locker floor — when a flash of red caught my eye.

Dripping red. Thick, dripping, red liquid oozing down the side of the locker door.

I gasped. At first I thought it was blood.

Then I quickly realized I was staring at paint. Bright red paint.

I scrambled to my feet — and read the scrawled message someone had painted on the door:

WHEN WILL THE CREEPS MEET?

"Whoa!" I cried out. I poked a finger in the paint and pulled it out smeared with red.

The paint was fresh. The letters dripped down the locker door. Someone had painted it just moments ago.

But who?

And why? Was it supposed to be a joke? What was the funny part?

It was all a mystery to me.

The bright red words glowed angrily out at me. I picked up my backpack and slammed the door.

I didn't have time to think about it all now. I had to get to class.

That night, the calls started early.

I finished my homework by eight thirty. I was in the den watching a basketball game on TV with my dad. The phone rang, and Dad picked up the cordless phone from the table beside him.

He muttered a few words, then shoved the phone toward me. "It's for you, Ricky."

I carried the phone out into the hall to get away from the noise of the basketball game. "Hello?"

"This is a Creep," a whispered voice replied. "When will the Creeps meet?"

I didn't say another word. I clicked the phone off and carried it back into the den.

I tried to watch the basketball game. But the phone kept ringing. One whispered voice after another.

"I'm a Creep. I saw your message."

"Are we ready to plant the seeds?"

"I'm a Creep. When are we meeting?"

This isn't funny, I thought. This is too strange to be funny.

17

As soon as school let out the next day, I ran to my locker. I stuffed the books I needed for homework into my backpack. Pulled on my blue parka. And ran out to the playground to meet Iris.

Was I a little pumped up?

You guessed it. I couldn't wait to take Iris shopping for baking supplies. I'll help her carry it all back to her house, I told myself. And then maybe she'll ask me to help her bake things for the bake sale.

Iris and I will work together. No girl had ever wanted to work together with me. When Brittany Hopper found out I was going to be her lab partner for frog dissection, she stayed home from school for two weeks!

I had to cut up my frog all by myself. And of course I made a disgusting mess of it.

But Iris was different. Iris was new.

Do they give prizes at bake sales?

Probably not. But if they did, I'm sure Iris and I could win one. And then the other kids in the school would see that I'm not such a loser.

These were my thoughts as I made my way to the back of the playground. I had big plans. Big, BIG plans.

But my plans never came true. No chance.

Because I never met Iris.

I turned to the school to look for her — and Wart, David, Jared, and Brenda jumped me from behind.

"Hey — let go!" I cried. I tried to squirm free.

But they swarmed over me and dragged me off the playground.

"Let go! What are you doing? Give me a break!" I screamed. I twisted and kicked. But I wasn't strong enough to break free.

They dragged me into the woods across from the playground. My sneakers scraped and slid over the carpet of wet, dead leaves.

They pulled me between the bare trees, trembling in the soft afternoon breeze. A scrawny squirrel scampered in front of us, searching the wintry ground for food.

"What are you going to do?" I cried. "Let me go! I mean it!"

They ignored my cries and dragged me through a clump of tall white weeds. "This way," David muttered.

He guided us to a line of high evergreen shrubs. Clumps of gray snow clung to the limbs of the shrubs.

Behind the evergreens, we were completely hidden from the street. With a hard tug, I pulled free.

Actually, I think they *let* me pull free.

I spun around. My eyes searched for the best way to escape. It wouldn't be easy. The snow-covered evergreen shrubs surrounded us on all four sides.

Wart and his friends stood tensely around me. They stared at me, as if waiting for me to speak.

"Why did you drag me here?" I demanded. I tried to sound calm, but my voice cracked. "What are you going to do to me?"

Their faces remained blank. Stern and serious. They didn't even laugh when my voice cracked.

Finally, Wart broke the tense silence. "We wouldn't harm you, Commander," he said.

I was sure I hadn't heard him correctly. "Excuse me?" I cried.

"We are the Creeps," Wart continued.

My mouth dropped open. "So you're the ones who have been calling me? And sending me messages?"

All four of them nodded solemnly. "Yes, Commander," Brenda said. She shook off some wet snowflakes that had fallen from the trees onto her long black hair.

"I should have known it was you," I muttered through clenched teeth.

"Yes. You should have known," Jared repeated.

"We called as soon as we got your message, Commander," David chimed in.

"What is this 'Commander' stuff?" I snapped. "Why are you calling me that?"

"We didn't guess that you were the Commander," Wart replied. "If we had known who you were, we never would have teased you and played mean jokes."

"Please accept our apology, Commander," Brenda added. "We are so sorry."

"You should have made yourself known to us sooner," David said.

"Yes. Now we must act quickly," Wart added.

"What are you talking about?" I screamed. "What is your problem?"

Were they trying to drive me crazy? What was this stupid new game about?

"I have to meet someone," I told them impatiently. "I don't have time for dumb games."

Some kids in my school were into fantasy games. They spent hours and hours role-playing characters in different fantasy worlds. You know. With dragons and elves and things.

But I never saw Wart and his pals playing those games.

So what on earth did they think they were doing now?

I knew it was all a stupid joke. It *had* to be a joke.

So why weren't they laughing? Why did they appear so grim?

Brenda trained her round dark eyes on me. "You no longer have to pretend," she said. "Now that we know you are the Commander, we must act quickly."

"We Creeps have so little time," Wart said, his eyes also locked on mine.

"It is urgent," David added. "That is why we have been calling you. To meet as soon as possible."

I saw the squirrel poking its head out from behind the evergreen shrub on the end. I wondered if I made a run for it, could I escape?

"Commander, we cannot understand why you have been delaying," Brenda said.

"Guys, this isn't funny —" I started.

They nodded solemnly. "We know," Jared said softly. "We have so little time to complete our mission."

Mission? Had they all totally lost it?

How long had it taken them to dream up this dumb joke? Did they really think I would buy it?

"What is the point of this?" I demanded.

"The Identity Seeds will grow stale in one week," Brenda said.

"We have so little time to plant them," David added fretfully. "So little time to turn everyone in the school into Creeps."

"Seeds? Plant seeds?" I laughed. What else could I do? I laughed in their faces. "Am I going crazy, or are you?" I asked.

"If we do not plant the seeds in time . . ." Wart started. But his voice trailed off before he finished his sentence.

Brenda picked up where Wart left off. "If we fail to plant the Identity Seeds," she said, keeping her eyes on me, "our mission will fail."

Wart placed a hand on my shoulder and gazed at me solemnly. "And of course, Commander, you *know* what will happen to you if the mission fails." He made a slicing motion across his throat.

A heavy silence fell over the woods. A burst of wind shook snow off the evergreens. I suddenly felt cold all over.

Brenda reached into her backpack. She pulled out a clear plastic bag and raised it toward me. "I have the Identity Seeds with me, Commander," she announced.

I studied the seeds inside the bag. They looked exactly like chocolate chips.

"As you know, Commander, every student must eat a seed," Wart said. "It takes only one seed to turn a human into a Creep."

"The Creeps must rule!" Jared declared loudly.

"Humans are the past!" Brenda cried, raising the bag of seeds high. "Creeps are the future!"

All four of them cheered. And as they cheered, they began to change — into MONSTERS!

"Creeps rule! Creeps rule!" they chanted.
I stared in horror as their faces twisted and their bodies began to change.

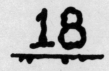

18

"Creeps rule! Creeps rule!" they chanted.

I stared in horror as their faces twisted and their bodies began to transform.

Bumps popped out all over their heads. Bumps about the size of quarters rose up on their arms and hands.

Their skin began to darken. In seconds, they were all bright purple. The big purple bumps trembled and shook on their skin.

Their faces stretched. Their hair disappeared into their purple skulls. Their eyes sank into their flat, purple heads.

Long, ropy tongues flicked from between jagged rows of teeth. Bumpy purple tongues, glistening as they whipped them from side to side.

I stared at them, unable to move, unable to run. Unable to take my eyes off the four creatures. Bumpy lizard creatures.

Creeps.

They grunted and wheezed. Their eyes rolled wetly. Their long snouts dripped. Their lizardy jaws snapped open and shut.

"NOOOO!" I cried out as Wart sprang at me.

I thought he was attacking.

But he scrambled past me — and grabbed the scrawny squirrel between both purple hands. Instantly, his jaws flew open, and he stuffed the squirrel inside.

He swallowed it without chewing. The furry tail slid down last.

His bumpy tongue licked his wet lips. "Sorry there wasn't enough to share." He grinned at the others.

"How was it?" Brenda hissed.

"A little dry," Wart replied.

"I don't like them with the skin on," Jared chimed in.

For some reason, that made them all laugh. Ugly, dry laughs that sounded like choking.

All four of them flicked out their long, bumpy tongues and slapped each other's tongues, as if slapping high fives.

I took a deep breath. My legs felt so weak, I thought I might fall to the ground. "I — I have to go now," I stammered.

In her purple fingers, Brenda raised the bag of seeds in front of my face. "Only one week left,

Commander," she said. "How will we plant them inside the students? We have waited so long for you. Do you have a plan?"

"Yes. My plan is to get out of here — now!" I replied.

I turned to leave. But they had me surrounded. Their wet eyes studied me. Their purple chests heaved noisily in and out. The bumps on their skin quivered.

Wart made a little bow, like a servant. "But if you leave, Commander, when will the Creeps meet again?" he asked softly.

"Yes. We must meet again soon. We must make a plan," David added solemnly.

"Before the week is out, every student at Harding Middle School must eat an Identity Seed," Brenda declared.

The others nodded.

"The Creeps will rule," Wart said softly. "The student humans will all become Creeps!"

Their tongues flicked out again and slapped each other in a four-tongued high five.

I've got to get away from them — now! I told myself.

I've got to report them. I've got to tell someone at school who they are — and what they're planning to do.

But — how?

19

I decided to play along with them. To stall. To act as serious as they were.

If they figure out that I'm not their Commander, they'll do something *horrible* to me! I realized.

I pictured the squirrel tail sliding down Wart's throat.

And I started to gag.

How can I get away from them? I wondered.

As soon as I escaped, I could report them to someone — to *anyone* who would listen!

"Brenda, let me see those seeds," I said, trying to sound as if I were giving an order. My voice came out strong and steady. But my hand trembled as I reached for the bag.

I took the bag and carefully unwrapped the twist-tie on top. Then I raised the bag to my face, studied the seeds for a long time, and took a deep sniff.

No. Definitely not chocolate chips.

The seeds had a faintly sour smell. Not terrible. But not sweet or chocolatey either.

"One for each kid," I murmured, eyeing them carefully. "One seed for each."

The four Creeps nodded their purple heads. "At least one for each student," Brenda said. "That's all it will take to turn them all into Creeps." She snapped her long rows of jagged teeth.

It's not going to happen, I decided.

No way.

I'm not going to let it happen. I'm going to get help. I'm going to stop them.

But first I had to get out of the woods.

"Well, we Creeps will meet again soon," I said. I handed the seed bag back to Brenda. "We must all think of the best plan. And then we will call each other, and pick a good time, and meet again."

I turned and took two steps toward the street.

That's as far as I got.

Wart's long, bumpy tongue wrapped around my neck. He turned me around by pulling in his tongue. "But, Commander — I *have* a good plan!" he declared.

"Good," I said, trying not to gag again. I could still feel the wet, bumpy tongue on my skin. "We will meet soon and talk about your plan."

"No — *now!*" Wart insisted. "Commander, we

must talk now. We can put my plan into action tomorrow morning!"

"Huh? Tomorrow?" I gasped. "I think we'd better wait a day," I started. "You see, if we all wait —"

They eyed me suspiciously. Their purple jaws opened and closed.

I turned back to Wart. "What's your plan?"

He took a deep, wheezing breath and began. "Tomorrow morning, we get to school very early. The lunchroom cooks all arrive early. They prepare lunch first thing in the morning."

"Yes. That gives the chocolate pudding plenty of time for the crust to harden!" I joked.

No one laughed.

"I've been studying the kitchen carefully," Wart continued. "After the cooks set out the food in the morning, they take a ten-minute break. That's our chance. If we sneak in during their break, we can plant the seeds in the lunchroom food."

"Everyone eats in the lunchroom. It's a school rule," David chimed in. "So every student will eat at least one seed."

"And by nighttime, they will no longer be humans. They will all be Creeps like us," Jared added.

"What do you think of my plan? Will it work?" Wart asked.

They all stared at me, waiting for my answer.

"The plan sounds pretty good," I said finally. I rubbed my chin, pretended I was thinking hard about it. "I will talk to you all tomorrow and let you know my decision."

Their lizardy faces drooped with disappointment. "Tomorrow?" Wart cried unhappily. "But we could *do* it tomorrow morning, Commander. We could plant the seeds, and by tomorrow night —"

I raised a hand to cut him off. "Tomorrow," I said firmly.

They were still grumbling to each other as I turned and hurried away. I expected one of them to grab me and pull me back. But this time, they let me go.

I edged through an opening in the evergreen shrubs. Then I started to jog. Between the bare, trembling trees. Across the street. And down the block toward my house.

What am I going to do? I asked myself as I ran.

I can't let them turn everyone in school into Creeps. I can't let them drop their Identity Seeds in the lunchroom food.

But how can I stop them?

If I tell them not to do it, they will figure out that I'm not their Commander. They will figure out that they made a mistake.

And then what? What will they do to me if they

find out I'm not a Creep? Will they gobble me up the way Wart swallowed that poor squirrel?

My side started to ache, but I kept running. I pictured all the kids in my school turning into bumpy, purple lizard creatures. I pictured them all in the woods, grabbing squirrels and swallowing them whole.

I pictured us all slouching around, slapping high fives with our tongues.

Yuck!

"What am I going to do?" I asked myself out loud.

I was the only one who knew about the Creeps — and the only one who could stop them.

And I had to act fast.

20

"Pass the mashed potatoes," Dad said with a mouthful of chicken. "And the biscuits, please."

I passed the food down the table. I took another drumstick from the bucket. Mom and Dad both work hard, so they don't have time to cook. They usually pick up something on the way home. Tonight it was a fried chicken bucket, with a bunch of side dishes.

They are always starving when they get home. There's no point in talking to them until they've finished their first helping. They can't even hear you over the sound of their chewing!

I really wasn't hungry. My stomach felt as if it were tied in tight knots. I kept staring at the chicken and picturing squirrel.

I waited until most of the chicken had been gobbled up. Then I took a deep breath and started my story.

"There's something I have to tell you," I said softly.

They both raised their eyes from their plates. Dad had a swirl of mashed potatoes on his cheek. Mom reached over and brushed it off with her fingers.

"Are you in trouble at school again, Ricky?" she asked sternly. "Have the kids been picking on you?"

"No. That's not it," I replied quickly. "I have to tell you something. I mean, I need your help. You see — these four kids —"

"Take a deep breath," Dad said. "Start at the beginning."

"Calm down," Mom added. "What's gotten you so wired?"

"Please — let me tell it!" I cried.

They both settled back and lowered their forks to the table.

"These four kids," I started again. "They're not really kids. I thought they were seventh-graders. But they're not. They're Creeps. They're not kids at all. I mean, they're new to the school. I never saw them before this year. But I thought . . ."

Mom and Dad exchanged glances. Dad opened his mouth to say something — then changed his mind.

"They came here with a mission," I told them. "They want to turn all the kids in school into Creeps. They have these Identity Seeds, a big bag of them. They're going to feed the seeds to all the kids."

I ran out of air. I hadn't taken a breath. I took a long one now, and continued my story.

"They think I'm a Creep, too. They think I'm their Commander. Because of a message I typed on the bottom of the school newspaper. They want me to help them turn all the kids into Creeps. Horrible monsters!"

I took another breath. I was so excited, so nervous, I felt as if my heart had jumped to my throat.

I leaned across the table and stared first at Mom, then at Dad. "We have to stop them!" I cried. "You have to help me. We can't let them turn everyone into Creeps. But what can we do? How can we let people know that they're not really kids? How can we stop them? You've got to help me. You've *got* to!"

I let out a long whoosh of air and dropped against the back of the chair. I struggled to slow down my racing heart.

My parents glanced at each other again. I could see the troubled expressions on their faces.

Dad was the first to speak. "Ricky," he said softly, "your mom and I are Creeps too."

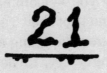

21

I gasped and nearly tumbled off my chair.

Mom and Dad burst out laughing.

"No. Actually we're Martians!" Dad declared.

"No way. We're not Martians," Mom argued. "We're werewolves!" She picked up a chicken bone and pretended to chomp on it like a wolf.

"We're Martian werewolves!" Dad cried. He tossed back his head and howled like a wolf.

Then they both laughed loudly again. They really thought they were a riot.

"You've got to take me seriously!" I pleaded.

For some reason, that made them laugh even harder. Dad actually had tears in his eyes from laughing so hard. He raised his napkin and dabbed at his eyes.

"Ricky, sometimes you come up with the greatest things," he said. He reached over and slapped my shoulder.

"What an imagination," Mom commented. She

shook her head. "You really should write that story down, Ricky. It could win a prize."

"But it isn't a story!" I cried. I jumped to my feet and angrily tossed my napkin onto my plate. "Why don't you believe me?"

"Oh, we believe you — Commander!" Dad exclaimed. "Commander of the Creeps!"

They both burst out laughing again.

I uttered an angry cry, turned, and stomped out of the dining room. I could still hear them laughing as I stormed up the stairs to my bedroom.

I slammed the door behind me. And shook my fists in the air.

I had to find some help. I had to make *someone* believe me.

I slumped onto my bed and just sat there for a long while, staring at the darkness outside the window. I waited for my heart to stop racing, for my mind to calm down.

But I couldn't get calm. My whole body tingled. My brain spun.

I grabbed the phone off my bedtable and punched in Iris's number. Iris will listen to me, I told myself. Iris will know I'm not making up a wild story.

The phone rang three times. Four. Five.

No one home?

"Come *on*, Iris!" I begged into the ringing receiver. "Be there!"

I let it ring twelve times before I hung up.

I slammed the phone back onto the bed table. After I calmed down a little, I sat down at my desk and tried to do my homework.

But I couldn't keep my mind on it.

At least the phone isn't ringing and ringing tonight, I told myself. The Creeps weren't calling me tonight.

They were waiting to hear from me. They were waiting to hear if I okayed Wart's plan to go to school early and plant the seeds in the lunchroom food.

I slammed my science textbook shut.

"I *will* go to school early," I said out loud.

But not to meet the four Creeps. Not to drop Identity Seeds into everyone's lunch.

I'll go to school early and talk to Ms. Crawford, the principal. I'll tell her the whole story. I'll tell her what the Creeps are planning to do at her school.

She'll help me stop them. I know she will.

My clock radio woke me half an hour earlier than usual. I clicked it off and listened to a soft patter against my bedroom window.

Staggering across the room, I peeked through the blinds. A gloomy gray day outside. Frozen rain dribbling down.

I yawned. I had tossed and twisted all night.

I got dressed quickly, pulling on a large red and

brown flannel shirt and baggy brown corduroy pants. I gulped down a fast breakfast of orange juice and corn flakes.

"You're up early this morning," Mom commented sleepily. She stood waiting for the coffeemaker to drip.

"Yeah. Got to go," I mumbled. I grabbed my parka and backpack and hurried out the back door.

I pulled my baseball cap down over my eyes and jogged through the cold, drizzling rain. Such a dreary day. Everything looked gray this morning. No bright color anywhere.

As I made my way to school, I practiced my speech to Ms. Crawford. I wanted to tell the story right. I wanted everything in the right order. I didn't want to leave out any important parts.

I passed a man in a gray rain slicker, out walking his Dalmatian. I didn't see anyone else on the street.

The school appeared empty when I arrived. The halls were silent. My wet shoes skidded over the floor.

I stepped into the front office. The room was empty. The two secretaries hadn't arrived yet. But I saw a light from the principal's office in back. And I heard a cough.

"Ms. Crawford, are you back there?" I called.

"Yes," she called back. "Who is it?"

I heard her chair scrape. And then she poked her white-haired head out of the office door. "Ricky?" She squinted at me in surprise. "You startled me. You're here awfully early, aren't you?"

"I — I need to talk to you," I stammered.

She motioned for me to step around the front counter and into her office. "What is the problem?" she asked, closing the door behind me.

"It's kind of a long story," I began.

Would she believe me?

22

Ms. Crawford always reminds me of a black-and-white movie. She has short, curly white hair, gray eyes, and a very pale face. And she always wears black — black pants suits and black skirts and tops.

I don't know how old she is. I think she's pretty old. But she's very lively and athletic. Sometimes she joins in during volleyball games in the gym.

I sat down in the stiff-backed chair in front of her desk. She moved some files aside and leaned across the desk toward me. "I'm glad you came by," she said, her smile fading.

"Huh? Really?"

"I've been meaning to talk to you, Ricky," she continued. "I understand there was some trouble at the car wash last Saturday."

She waited for me to say something. But I didn't know what to say.

"I've been told that you started a water fight last Saturday," Ms. Crawford said sternly.

"*Me?*" I cried. "I didn't start it! I — I —"

She motioned with one hand for me to be silent. "Mr. Wartman — Richard's father — called me to complain. He said that the inside of his car was totally soaked. He told me that —"

"That's who I want to talk to you about," I interrupted. I could see that this conversation was not going as I had planned. I decided I'd better jump in as fast as possible.

"I want to talk to you about Wart," I said. "I mean, Richard. He's not a kid, see. He told me. He's a Creep."

Ms. Crawford's mouth dropped open. She blinked at me.

"And you know his three friends?" I blurted out. "They're Creeps too. They're monsters. Purple monsters."

Ms. Crawford twisted her face into a frown. "Ricky —" she started.

"No — really!" I insisted. "They're monsters. They call themselves Creeps! They told me so themselves. I *saw* them! Wart ate a squirrel! He's a Creep!"

This wasn't going over well. I could see that by the deepening furrows in Ms. Crawford's forehead. It wasn't the way I'd planned to tell the story. But it was too late now. I had to get it all out.

"I'm their Commander," I told the principal. "At least, they *think* I'm their Commander. But I'm not really. And they —"

Ms. Crawford jumped to her feet. "Ricky — are you okay?" she asked.

"They want to plant seeds and turn the whole school into Creeps," I continued frantically. "They want . . ."

She stepped around her desk and placed a hand on my forehead. "Do you have a temperature? You feel a little warm."

She moved back and studied my face. "Would you like to see the nurse? She usually comes in early."

"No. Not the nurse!" I cried. "You don't understand. We can't let anyone eat the lunchroom food! Because they're monsters!"

Ms. Crawford scratched the top of her head. "Should I send you home?" she asked. "Do you feel sick? I could have someone take you home." She reached for the phone. "Are your parents still home? I could call them."

"No — please!" I jumped to my feet. "I'm okay. Really."

She wasn't going to believe me. No way I could get her to listen to me.

"Just a joke," I said, backing to the door. "Just a joke. Really. I'm sorry about Mr. Wartman's car. It was an accident. The hose just slipped."

I fumbled for the door. Pushed it open. Backed out.

"Ricky, wait," Ms. Crawford called. "I really think you should see the nurse. Just talk to her.

You seem very excited. Perhaps if you talk to her . . ."

"I'm fine. Really," I insisted.

I turned and ran through the front office and out the door.

Into the long, empty hallway.

My heart flip-flopping in my chest, I turned the corner — and bumped into Wart and his three friends.

"Ohh!" I let out a startled cry. "What are *you* doing here?"

"Glad you joined us, Commander," Wart said in a whisper. His eyes glanced up and down the hall. "Let's go."

"Go? Go where?" I demanded.

"To the lunchroom," he replied.

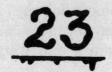

23

I turned and looked for Ms. Crawford. But she had stayed in her office. The long hall stood empty.

Wart and David moved to my sides. Brenda led the way to the stairs that went down to the lunchroom and the kitchen. Jared walked close behind me.

They had me surrounded. I had no choice. I had to go with them.

When we reached the bottom of the stairs, I could see the open doors to the kitchen. Bright white light poured out to the hall.

I took a deep breath.

What was that smell? Tuna casserole?

I could hear women's voices, the cooks working away at the stoves.

With Brenda leading the way, the five of us moved silently to the kitchen doorway. Now I could hear the clatter of pots and the hiss of something cooking on the stove. A woman coughed. Another one laughed.

Brenda turned suddenly, and I nearly walked into her. She shoved something into my hand.

The plastic bag of seeds.

"You may have the honor, Commander," she whispered solemnly. "You may hide the seeds in the food."

"Uh . . . well . . ." I pressed my back against the tile wall. I didn't want to go in there. I didn't want the honor of planting the seeds.

"Maybe we should come back later," I suggested. "Remember I suggested that we wait? I told you to wait until —"

"We have no choice," Jared whispered. "We know you want the mission to succeed."

"Good luck," Brenda said softly.

David and Jared gave me a hard push into the kitchen.

Squeezing the bag of seeds between my hands, I blinked in the bright light. I could see three women in white uniforms and white aprons. They stood across the big room at the stoves against the wall.

They had their backs to me. Tall soup pots bubbled and steamed on the stoves.

I swallowed hard. If one of them turned around, she'd see me instantly.

I slid beside a cabinet near the doorway. Ahead

91

of me stood a long, shiny aluminum counter. Enormous trays of food stood cooling on the counter. I saw a big tray of macaroni and cheese, a tray of steamed broccoli, a huge tray of tuna casserole.

I guessed it would take about ten steps to reach the counter. So close!

I could probably dive to the counter, pour the seeds out into one of the big food trays, and run out the door in less than ten seconds.

Even if one of the cooks turned around, I could accomplish the mission and be out of there before she could even cry out.

What am I thinking? I asked myself, pressing against the side of the cabinet.

I don't WANT to accomplish the mission!

I glanced back to the kitchen doorway. All four Creeps huddled there, watching me. They waved their hands frantically, motioning me to get on with it.

I had no choice. No way to escape.

I had to go ahead and plant the seeds.

I sucked in a deep breath and held it. Then, my eyes on the white-uniformed backs of the three cooks, I crept up quickly to the long food counter.

I stopped a few feet away. In front of me on the counter stood an enormous square metal pan of macaroni and cheese. It was steaming hot, fresh from the oven. The tangy cheese smell floated up to me.

I can't do this! I decided. I can't!

I turned back. The four Creeps leaned into the doorway, blocking my escape. All four of them were signaling wildly for me to pour the seeds.

I turned back to the macaroni tray.

I raised the seed bag.

I pulled open the top.

They're watching me, I knew. They're all watching. I have to do this. Or else they will know that I'm not their Commander.

I have to go ahead with it.

But then — in a flash — I had an idea.

24

I held the seed bag in one hand from the bottom. I raised it in front of me.

I turned and flashed the four Creeps a thumbs-up sign. Then I took a step toward the food counter.

Another step.

And I pretended to trip over something.

I stumbled forward. My hands shot up. And the seed bag flew into the air.

I faked a frantic attempt to catch it as I went down.

But the bag hit the side of the aluminum counter. Turned upside down. And dropped to the floor, spilling the seeds all over the floor. I watched them roll in all directions.

The bag lay on its side in front of me. Empty.

Yessss! I thought happily. I've done it! I've destroyed their plan!

I forced an unhappy expression on my face.

And scrambled on my hands and knees out the kitchen door.

Wart pulled me up and dragged me away from the open doorway.

I shook my head sadly. "Sorry," I murmured. "I'm so sorry. I have failed you all." I pretended to be near tears. "Really. I'm so sorry."

"No problem," Jared replied.

He pulled another bag of seeds from his coat pocket and slapped it into my hand.

"We always carry a spare," Brenda whispered. "You never know when you'll need more Identity Seeds."

"Uh . . . that's lucky," I replied.

"Now go do it!" Wart cried softly, slapping me on the back. "This time you will not fail, Commander."

The four of them pushed me back through the doorway.

I blinked, waiting for my eyes to adjust to the bright kitchen lights. The three cooks were still working at the stoves. They still had their backs to me.

I crept up to the food counter and peered down at the huge tray of simmering macaroni. I had the seed bag gripped tightly in my right hand. The little bag felt as if it weighed a hundred pounds!

I raised the seed bag over the steaming macaroni.

Glanced back to the doorway. All four of the Creeps leaned into the opening, their eyes locked on me.

I turned back to the food counter. Raised the bag higher over the macaroni tray.

I have no choice, I told myself. I have to do this now.

I poured the whole bag of seeds over the top of the macaroni and cheese. Then I turned quickly to the door. And tiptoeing silently, started to sneak out of the kitchen.

"Stir them!" Brenda whispered. She made a stirring motion with her hand.

"Huh?" I stopped a few feet from the door.

"Stir the seeds in!" she whispered urgently. "You've got to hide them!"

"Oh. Right."

I turned and crept back up to the big tray of macaroni and cheese. I picked up a long wooden spoon and stirred the seeds into the macaroni. Then I turned to sneak back out.

I took three steps — when two strong hands grabbed my shoulders roughly from behind. "What are *you* doing in here, young man?" a woman barked.

25

The hands spun me around. I stared up into the angry face of Mrs. Marshall. "What are you doing in here?" she repeated.

Mrs. Marshall is the *nice* cook. She's our favorite. She always kids around with everyone at lunchtime when she dishes out the food.

But she wasn't kidding around now. She knew I didn't belong in the kitchen.

Her black curls pressed against her hair net. She tilted her head, hands in her white apron pocket, waiting for me to answer her question.

I glanced to the door. Saw the four Creeps peeking in.

"Mrs. Marshall," I whispered. "Don't serve the macaroni."

She squinted at me. "Huh? Speak up, young man."

"Don't serve the macaroni," I whispered, a little louder. I couldn't say it much louder. Wart and his three friends would hear me. "Please — don't let anyone eat the macaroni," I begged.

"What are you saying?" she demanded loudly. "Why are you whispering?"

"Don't serve the macaroni," I repeated, still in a whisper. "It's poisoned!"

She uttered an angry groan. "Young man, our macaroni is delicious," she declared. "I'm so sick and tired of jokes about our food."

"She's right!" Another cook, Mrs. Davis, chimed in from across the room. She waved a long mixing spoon at me. "We make good, wholesome food here. It's like home-cooked. And we're tired of all the horrible jokes."

"We have feelings, you know," Mrs. Marshall added.

"We use real cheese in the macaroni," Mrs. Davis called, still waving her spoon. "None of that artificial stuff. And real macaroni noodles."

"That's right!" the third cook called. She was new. I didn't know her name. "Give him a taste, Alice. Give him a taste of the macaroni. He'll see how good it is."

Mrs. Marshall leaned over me. "Good idea. Would you like a little bowl of macaroni?" She stepped over to the food counter.

"Try it. You won't make any more jokes," Mrs. Davis said.

Mrs. Marshall started to spoon out a little bowl of macaroni for me.

I backed up toward the door. "No. Please. No thank you," I sputtered.

I reached the doorway. "I . . . I had a big breakfast," I told them.

I turned and ran out. And bumped into the four Creeps. They all cheered.

"Commander . . . you have done it!" Wart cried happily. "You have planted the seeds!"

They cheered again, and clapped and slapped me on the back. All four of them were grinning their heads off.

"Now we just have to wait till this afternoon," Brenda declared. "This school will be crawling with Creeps!"

26

I didn't go near the lunchroom at lunchtime. I hid in a stairwell instead. My stomach was growling, but I didn't care.

I couldn't bear to see all the kids gobbling down the macaroni. Swallowing the little seeds that would turn them into squirrel-eating Creeps.

A school full of purple lizard monsters, I thought miserably. And all my fault . . . my fault.

All afternoon, I didn't hear a word my teacher said. Iris tried to talk to me, but I pretended to be listening really hard to the teacher.

I sat at my desk, studying the other kids. Watching for signs that they were changing. Waiting for the seeds I had planted to do their evil.

But I didn't see anything odd. No bumpy purple skin. No long, flicking tongues.

The kids all appeared normal.

After school, the four Creeps were waiting for

me in the playground. They surrounded me and led me to our hiding place in the woods across the street.

Wart angrily kicked a stone out of his way. David and Jared were muttering unhappily and shaking their heads.

"It didn't work," Brenda said softly. "The seeds didn't work. No one changed."

"What went wrong?" Wart asked. "What could have gone wrong?"

They all stared at me.

Suddenly, I knew the answer. I knew exactly why none of the kids had turned into Creeps. "No one ate the macaroni," I blurted out.

I could have *kicked* myself. Why did I tell them? Why did I tip them off?

They narrowed their eyes at me. "Huh?"

"No one *ever* eats the macaroni," I said. I'd already started. I had to explain. "It's sort of a school rule. The macaroni hasn't been touched by anyone in years and years!"

All four of them groaned.

Wart stepped up to me and stared at me suspiciously. "How do you know that, Commander?" he demanded. "You arrived here only a few days before we did. So how do you know that the macaroni hasn't been eaten in years?"

I had to think fast. If they discovered that I wasn't a Creep, they'd probably disintegrate me — or eat me — or something!

"Uh . . . one of the kids in my class told me," I replied. I lowered my head. "I should have remembered sooner. I have failed you. Our mission is a failure."

"No, it isn't," Brenda chimed in. "I have more seeds — and a new plan. A better plan."

The other Creeps turned to her. "Tell us your plan," Jared demanded. "We don't have much time before the seeds lose their power."

"It's simple," Brenda replied with a shrug. "We bake the seeds into cookies. Then we hand out the cookies for free at the school bake sale on Saturday."

"Excellent idea!" David cried.

"Yaaaay!" Wart and Jared cheered.

"Everyone gets a free cookie," Brenda said, grinning an evil grin. "And everyone becomes a Creep."

Brenda's grin made me feel cold all over. I swallowed hard. My mouth suddenly felt so dry.

I knew that her plan would work. I knew that no one in my school could pass up a free cookie.

What can I do? I asked myself. How can I stop them?

They all turned to me. "Shall we bake the cookies, Commander?" Wart demanded. "Shall we put Brenda's plan into action?"

I stared back at them. They were eagerly waiting for my answer. I wondered if they could see my knees shaking.

"Well..." I took a deep breath. I had to try something. I had to think of *something* to stop them.

"I don't like Brenda's plan," I said, trying to keep my voice low and steady. "I think we must prepare the seeds for a later time. I think we should bury the seeds in the ground and see if they sprout. That way, we'll have lots and *lots* of seeds!"

I know. I know. It was a really lame idea.

But it was the only thing that popped into my mind.

Would they buy it? I wondered.

Would they forget about Brenda's plan and go along with it?

Would they agree to bury the seeds?

No way.

It took me only a few seconds to realize I had made the worst mistake of my life.

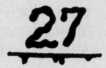

27

"Bury the seeds?" Brenda cried. "*Bury* them?"

The four of them moved in closer. They formed a tight circle around me.

I glanced nervously around, searching the woods for the best path to escape. But they had me trapped.

"Are you sure you are our Commander?" Wart demanded.

David and Jared sneered at me. "A Creep Commander would never tell us to *bury* the Identity Seeds," Jared said menacingly.

Wart stuck his face up close to mine. "Prove you are our Commander," he ordered.

"Yes. Prove you are a Creep!" David cried.

"Prove it! Prove it!" All four of them began to chant.

I gasped and tried to back away. But they had me surrounded.

"Prove it! Prove it!"

And as they chanted, they began to change

once again. Their skin grew bumpy and turned bright purple. Their hair slid into their heads, and their jaws stretched into long, toothy snouts.

"Prove it! Prove it!" they chanted. "Prove that you're a Creep!"

I stared at them, unable to move, unable to run. What could I do?

"Prove you're a Creep!" they demanded. "Prove it — now!"

Eyes flashing wildly, purple bumps quivering all over their bodies, they slithered toward me.

And I knew I was doomed.

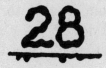

28

"Prove it! Prove it!"

Their long, bumpy tongues flicked at me as they chanted.

"Prove that you're one of us! Change now! Let us see you change like us!"

I swallowed hard. They were chanting for me to change, staring, waiting.

They'd have to wait a long, long time!

"Change! Change! Change!"

They were about to learn the truth about me.

I decided I had to confess. And beg them for mercy. "Uh . . . guys . . . ?" I started.

But then a girl's shout rose over the chanting of the Creeps. "Stop at once!" she cried.

We all turned to see Iris come running out from behind a tall evergreen. The four Creeps uttered grunts of surprise. Their eyes rolled wildly in their purple lizard heads.

"I am the Commander's second-in-command!"

Iris declared, her long earrings jangling wildly. "I am his sergeant!"

The Creeps pulled their long, bumpy tongues into their snouts. They stared at Iris, suddenly silent.

"The Commander and I do not choose to transform now," Iris told them sternly. "We do not have time. We must bake the cookies now. We must prepare the seeds for the bake sale."

"Yaaaay!" The Creeps cheered Iris.

"Thank you, Sergeant," Brenda said. "I am glad you like my plan."

"Your plan will work," Iris replied. "We will turn the whole school into Creeps like us. Quickly. Let us hurry to my house and bake the cookies."

The four lizard creatures offered up another cheer. They slapped tongues. Then they quickly began to change back into kids.

The purple on their skin faded. The quivering bumps slid into their skin. Their snouts shrunk and their faces twisted back into the faces of the kids I knew.

As they changed back, I leaned close to Iris and whispered in her ear. "Iris — you're really one of them?"

"Yes, Commander," she replied, keeping her eyes on the four Creeps. "Do not worry. This new plan will not fail."

I opened my mouth to say something, but no sound came out. I couldn't believe it. Iris — a Creep!

We began making our way through the woods. Iris led the way to her house.

The afternoon sun was sinking behind the bare trees. The air suddenly felt cold and heavy. I couldn't stop the chills that rolled down my back.

I'd had a close call in the woods. Iris had saved me. But I knew my troubles weren't over.

I was in terrible danger.

So were all the kids at school.

We stepped into Iris's kitchen. Why did Iris save me? I wondered. She knows I'm not one of them. She knows I'm not a Creep.

So, why did she rescue me from the other four Creeps?

As the four of them took out flour and eggs and other ingredients, I pulled Iris aside. "You know I'm not a Creep," I whispered. "Why did you rescue me?"

"I'm not a Creep either," she whispered back. "But I saw you were in big trouble."

"How did you know — ?" I started. I glanced back into the kitchen to make sure the Creeps weren't watching us.

"You were supposed to meet me on the playground — remember?" Iris whispered. "I saw them drag you into the woods. I followed you. I heard everything. And I saw everything."

"Well, thanks for saving me," I replied. "But now you are in danger too."

She nodded. "I know. But I had to save you — didn't I?"

"How are we going to save the rest of the school?" I whispered.

"Good question," Iris replied. "We have to bake the cookies now. We don't have a choice. When we get to the bake sale, we'll figure out a way to keep kids from eating them."

"Yeah. Sure." I rolled my eyes.

How would we keep kids from grabbing up free cookies?

How?

29

On Saturday morning, Iris and I and the four Creeps carried our big trays of cookies into the gym.

What a crowd!

Every kid in school was there. They were running back and forth, carrying trays of baked goods to the tables. Talking and laughing and kidding around.

A podium with a microphone had been set up under the basket at one end of the gym. The long row of tables stretched from one wall to the other.

As Iris and I walked to the tables, the four Creeps stayed close at our sides. Protecting the cookies. Watching our every move.

The cookies with the Identity Seeds inside were piled high on the two trays. We had baked hundreds of them. More than enough for every kid in school.

We passed by a group of kids gobbling down brownies. At the near table, Ms. Williamson, our teacher, was busy cutting slices in a cheesecake. I saw dozens of plates of cookies spread over the tables.

Signs were posted, giving the prices. Just about everything cost a dollar. Nothing was free.

Our cookies were the only free items.

How could I stop kids from taking them? How could I make sure that no one ate them?

We headed to the tables. But Wart stepped in front of us. "Start giving them out now," he urged.

"Yes. There's no reason to wait," Brenda agreed. "Let's pass out the cookies. The gym is totally jammed with kids. In a few minutes, we'll have dozens of new Creeps."

Wart grabbed for the tray.

David and Jared pulled the plastic wrapping off the cookies.

I've got to act — now! I knew.

But what could I do?

As Wart lifted the cookie tray from my hands, I had an idea.

I dodged past him. Swung my way around a group of chocolate cake eaters. Leaped behind the podium where Tasha was about to make a welcoming speech. And grabbed the microphone.

"Attention! Attention, everyone!" I screamed.

A loud squeal from the speakers got everyone's attention. My panicky voice echoed off the high gym walls.

"Don't eat the free cookies!" I shouted. "Please — listen to me, everyone! Don't eat the free cookies! You will all become monsters! Bumps will grow all over you, and you'll look like purple lizard creatures! And . . . and . . . you'll eat squirrels whole!"

Everyone laughed. The laughter drowned out my desperate words.

"You've *got* to believe me!" I shrieked into the microphone. I could see Wart and David running toward the podium. "You've *got* to! Stay away from the free cookies!"

The laughter rose up until I couldn't hear myself.

"Get away from that mike!" Tasha screamed. She tried to grab the microphone from my hands.

Two teachers rushed up to pull me away.

"Sicky Ricky! Sicky Ricky!" Tasha started to chant. And then the rest of the huge crowd of kids joined in.

"Sicky Ricky! Sicky Ricky!" The gym rang with their chanting and wild laughter.

I could feel my heart sink to my stomach.

"Sicky Ricky! Sicky Ricky!" The chanting made me feel as if my head was about to burst.

I wanted to cover my ears. I wanted to run. I wanted to disappear.

How can I save them if they're just going to laugh at me? I wondered. What can I do if they refuse to listen to me?

And then I had another idea. An even more desperate plan than grabbing the microphone and begging them.

"Sicky Ricky! Sicky Ricky!" Tasha led the chanting.

I tried to ignore the laughing, shouting voices. I knew I had only a few seconds to act.

Would my plan work?

Probably not. But it was the only thing my panicked brain could come up with.

I'll gobble down all the cookies myself, I decided.

I'll grab the trays and eat all the cookies — and save everyone in the school.

With a wild leap, I pushed past a bunch of chanting kids. I grabbed the tray of cookies from Wart's hands. And I opened my mouth to start swallowing them down.

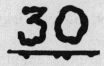

30

"Ow!"

I cried out when something smacked me in the forehead.

I wasn't hurt. Just startled.

I reached a hand up and felt something wet and gooey. Someone had thrown a piece of chocolate pie.

Kids laughed. Tasha ran up and flashed my picture.

"Hey — !" I cried out angrily.

"Sicky Ricky! Sicky Ricky!" some kids chanted.

"Ricky Rat! Ricky Rat!" I heard other kids sing.

Someone threw a brownie. I ducked and it sailed over my shoulder. I nearly dropped the tray of cookies. Laughing, Tasha snapped another photo.

"What's *wrong* with you?" I shouted. "I'm trying to save you!"

"Sicky Ricky! Sicky Ricky!"

"Ricky Rat! Ricky Rat!"

Don't they realize what danger they're in? I asked myself. Why are they making fun of me? Why do they *always* make fun of me? I'm only trying to save them!

"Sicky Ricky! Sicky Ricky!"

Someone hit me in the chest with a gooey slice of cheesecake.

I raised the cookie tray. I've got to save them, I told myself. I have to ignore all the teasing and chanting and laughing. I've got to save them all!

Wart and Brenda closed in on me. "Commander, what are you waiting for?" Wart asked. "Pass out the cookies."

"Ignore their chanting," Brenda said. "Once they eat the cookies, they will all be Creeps. You will be their leader. They will all be your slaves!"

I've got to save them, I repeated to myself. Got to save them. Got to save them . . .

I turned to Brenda. "Huh? What did you say?"

"I *said* they will all be your slaves!" Brenda shouted over the chanting and laughter.

My slaves?

My *slaves*?

My slaves???

I ducked as someone tossed another slice of cheesecake at me.

"Sicky Ricky! Sicky Ricky!" they chanted.

"Here — Tasha — have a cookie!" I cried. I held the tray out to her and watched her take it.

"Have a cookie! Free cookies!" I shouted at the top of my lungs.

Hands grabbed eagerly for the cookies. I moved quickly, happily around the gym, handing out cookies to every kid.

"Plenty for everyone!" I shouted. "That's right — they're free! And they're the *best*! Free cookies! Free cookies! That's it, everyone! Gobble them up! One for everyone! Free cookies!"

I flashed my four friends a thumbs-up. And I took a cookie for myself.

Not bad. A little chewy, but very sweet.

I gazed around the gym. Watched everyone chewing up the free cookies.

From now on, I told myself, *things are going to be very different around here.*

And I can't wait!

About R.L. Stine

R.L. STINE is the most popular author in America. He is the creator of the *Goosebumps*, *Give Yourself Goosebumps*, *Fear Street*, and *Ghosts of Fear Street* series among other popular books. He has written more than one hundred scary novels for kids. Bob lives in New York City with his wife, Jane, teenage son, Matt, and dog, Nadine.

Add *more*

to your collection . . .
A chilling preview of
what's next from
R.L. STINE

BEWARE, THE SNOWMAN

22

All three of us stopped at the end of the road and stared at the cabin up ahead. The late afternoon sun had fallen behind the trees. The snow billowed in front of us in shades of gray.

To the left of the cabin, I saw a row of low evergreen shrubs, covered in snow.

"I'll hide behind those shrubs," I told Rolonda and Eli. "You run up to the cabin and keep Conrad and the wolf from seeing me."

"This isn't going to work," Eli muttered, his eyes on the cabin.

"It's getting kind of dark," Rolonda fretted. "Maybe we should come back in the morning."

"Maybe we should forget the whole idea," Eli suggested. I saw his chin quiver. He shuddered.

"Hey — you promised!" I exclaimed. "A promise is a promise — right?"

They didn't reply. They both stared across the gray snow to the dark cabin up ahead.

"I came this far. I'm not going back," I said sharply. "Are you going to help me or not?

I gasped when I heard a low growl from the cabin. The wolf must have heard us or smelled us.

I knew it would come running out any second.

"Come *on*!" I urged in a loud whisper. And I took off for the snow-covered shrubs.

I ducked out of view just as Conrad and the wolf burst out of the cabin.

"Hello — !" Rolonda cried to Conrad.

"Hi!" Eli echoed."

I watched Rolonda and Eli go running up to Conrad.

The wolf lowered its head, watching them carefully.

I saw Rolonda and Eli, both talking at once, chattering at Conrad. I couldn't hear what they said.

They're doing it! I told myself, my heart pounding. They're keeping his attention.

Time for me to move.

Time for me to make a run for it.

I could hear Rolonda talking to Conrad. I glanced over the top of the bush. The wolf had its back to me.

Conrad was scratching his gray hair, listening to Rolonda. I couldn't see his expression. But I imagined he was very confused and surprised.

I knew he didn't get any visitors.

He must be wondering what Rolonda and Eli were doing up here!"

I forced all of these thoughts from my mind.

It was time for me to make a run for it.

I took a deep breath.

Then, still crouching, I began to run.

My legs felt like Jell-O. My boots sank into the deep snow.

Ducking my head, I darted up the steep mountainside.

Up, up.

I had just passed the bushes when I heard Conrad's angry shout — "Hey, *wait!*"

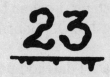

23

I stopped so suddenly, I fell over backward!

I landed hard. The snow seemed to fly up in my face, sweep over me, surround me. Everything went white.

I'm caught, I realized.

My plan didn't work.

I stood up and turned to face Conrad.

To my shock, he wasn't coming after me. He and the wolf were running downhill. Chasing after Rolonda and Eli.

I heard the wolf utter a high growl. Then they disappeared around a curve.

I stood frozen in place, staring at the spot where they had just been.

Would Conrad harm Rolonda and Eli?

Should I run after them and try to help them?

No. I had to keep going.

This was the plan. This was my chance.

Taking another deep breath, I turned and continued to run up the mountainside. The climb was steep for a while. So steep I wasn't sure I could make it.

But then the ground leveled off. I found myself on a wide ledge. The ledge was slick. My boots slipped on the ice.

I pressed my back against the mountain wall.

And gazed up at the ice cave.

Yes!

There it stood above me. A cave as tall as a building. Smooth and glassy, it reflected the clouds in the sky above it.

I couldn't see the entrance from here. I was staring at one of the sides.

The ledge narrowed as it curled up to the cave.

I kept my back pressed against the wall and slowly — step by step — inched my way toward the top.

"Don't look down!" I murmured out loud.

But as soon as I said it, I had to look.

It was a deep drop from the ledge to the ground far, far below.

If I slipped and fell . . .

I'm not going to slip and fall! I told myself.

A deep, rumbling sound made me jump!

I grabbed the mountainside with both hands to keep from falling.

The ledge trembled beneath me.

Another low rumble made me cry out in fear.

The ledge trembled again. The whole mountain seemed to shake!

The sound came from the cave up above.

Is something moving up there? I wondered.

Or is it the normal sound of a mountaintop in the wind?

I gathered my courage and moved forward. Inch by inch.

I had come this far. I refused to retreat now.

The ledge grew narrower, slipperier, as it curved around.

Another rumbling noise made me gasp.

Somehow I held on. And followed the ledge around.

It seemed to take forever. But a short while later, the cave opening came into view.

And a short while after that, I saw the most terrifying sight of my life.

24

I didn't see it at first.

First, I saw the layer of solid ice that covered the ledge. The glassy cave rose up behind the ledge. The gaping entrance to the cave was blacker than the darkest night.

I stood staring into the darkness. Trying to catch my breath. Trying to slow my pounding heart.

Clouds reflected in the glassy ice drifted rapidly to the right. They made the cave appear to move.

Sharply pointed icicles stabbed down from the roof of the cave opening. They reminded me of sharpened teeth about to close.

I stared into the black cave opening and waited. Waited to see if anything would appear.

I didn't have to wait long.

A rumble as loud as thunder made the ledge quake.

Afraid I might slip off, I dropped to my knees.

The rumble grew to a roar.

And a tall, white figure lumbered out from the blackness of the cave entrance. An enormous snowman!

I gasped — and stared in horror as the mountain of snow moved toward me. "Nooooo!" I wailed.

I forgot where I was. Forgot I was perched on a narrow ice ledge.

And started to back up, to back away from the tall creature.

And I slipped.

Slipped off the ledge.

And felt myself fall.

25

My hands shot up.

Shot up and dug into the ledge.

I gripped the icy ledge. Held on. Held on.

With a terrified groan, I scrambled back up to safety. Trembling. My entire body shaking. My breath escaping in short, frantic gasps.

I huddled on my knees on the icy ledge and watched the snowman as it glared down at me. Its blood-red scarf flapped in the wind. Its round, black eyes were as big as doorknobs. Its dark mouth turned down in a fierce, angry sneer.

And the scar. The scar cut deeply into the side of its round head, long and curling, like a black snake.

"Ohhhhhh." I uttered another moan as its tree branch arms reached for me.

I shivered in a sudden, deep cold. A cold I'd never felt before. I could see frozen waves floating from the snowman's wide body.

And then the big, round head tilted. The black eyes bulged even wider.

And the snowman bellowed in a deep roar of a voice: *"WHO ARE YOU?"*

I trembled in the waves of cold that floated off its body.

It talks!

The stories Rolonda and Eli told me are true. It's all true.

Its round eyes locked on mine, the big snowman moved closer. Closer.

I wanted to stand up. I wanted to run.

But it had me frozen there.

I couldn't stand. I couldn't back up. I couldn't escape from it.

"WHO ARE YOU?" the snowman bellowed again. And the whole mountain shook.

"I — I — " My voice came out in a quivering squeak.

"Please — " I managed to choke out. "Please — I didn't mean to bother you. I — "

"WHO ARE YOU?" the huge snow creature thundered again.

"My name?" I squeaked. "My name is Jaclyn. Jaclyn DeForest."

The snowman's tree branch arms shot up. Its dark mouth gaped open in surprise.

"SAY IT AGAIN," it ordered.

I shivered in the waves of cold. "Jaclyn DeForest," I repeated in my tiny, frightened voice.

The snowman stared down at me in silence for a long while. It lowered its arms to its round, white sides.

"*DO YOU KNOW WHO I AM?*" it demanded.

I swallowed hard. The question took me totally by surprise. I opened my mouth to answer, but no sound came out.

"*DO YOU KNOW WHO I AM?*" the snowman thundered.

"No," I squeaked. "Who are you?"

He's Got a Heart of Cold!

Goosebumps®

Jaclyn can't believe her Aunt Greta made
her move to the isolated mountain town
of Sherpia. The only thing the town has
is a bunch of creepy looking snowmen...
and one talking snowman.
The townspeople say he's dangerous.
Aunt Greta says he's a monster.
The snowman claims he's Jaclyn's father!
Could it be true? If so,
who's her snow*mom*?

BEWARE, THE SNOWMAN

Goosebumps #51
by R.L. Stine

Find it at a bookstore near you!

R.L. STINE
GIVE YOURSELF
Goosebumps®

This Evil Genie Has Got You in a Jam!

You and your brother are heading home from school. You grab a can of soda–and when you open it...a Genie pops out! Now you have three wishes. When you want to fly, she turns you into a vulture. When you want to be a famous star, she turns you into a TV monster. Now you have one wish left–and you're kind of wishing you were never born–but be careful, you-know-who can definitely arrange that!

What will you wish for? Choose from more than 20 spooky endings!

Give Yourself Goosebumps #13
Scream of the Evil Genie
by R.L. Stine

Coming soon to a bookstore near you!

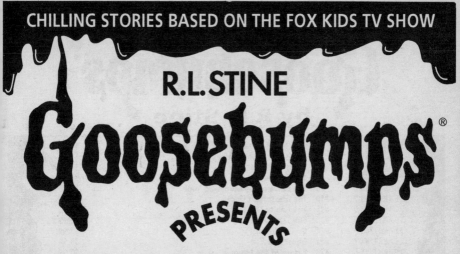

R.L. STINE

Goosebumps®

PRESENTS

TV EPISODE #8

It's going to take more than practice to make Samantha a good basketball player. So when a mysterious woman grants Samantha three wishes, she uses one to make herself stronger on the court. But instead, everyone on her team gets weaker! Then Sam wishes her loudmouthed enemy, Judith, would disappear. And she does—along with the rest of the town! Can Sam stop all of the horrible things that have happened...with just one wish?

Goosebumps Presents TV Episode #8

Be Careful What You Wish For

by R.L. Stine

With 8 pages of full-color photos from the show!

Look for it in a bookstore near you!

GET Goosebumps®
by R.L. Stine

❏ BAB45365-3	#1	Welcome to Dead House	$3.99
❏ BAB45366-1	#2	Stay Out of the Basement	$3.99
❏ BAB45367-X	#3	Monster Blood	$3.99
❏ BAB45368-8	#4	Say Cheese and Die!	$3.99
❏ BAB45369-6	#5	The Curse of the Mummy's Tomb	$3.99
❏ BAB49445-7	#10	The Ghost Next Door	$3.99
❏ BAB49450-3	#15	You Can't Scare Me!	$3.99
❏ BAB47742-0	#20	The Scarecrow Walks at Midnight	$3.99
❏ BAB47743-9	#21	Go Eat Worms!	$3.99
❏ BAB47744-7	#22	Ghost Beach	$3.99
❏ BAB47745-5	#23	Return of the Mummy	$3.99
❏ BAB48354-4	#24	Phantom of the Auditorium	$3.99
❏ BAB48355-2	#25	Attack of the Mutant	$3.99
❏ BAB48350-1	#26	My Hairiest Adventure	$3.99
❏ BAB48351-X	#27	A Night in Terror Tower	$3.99
❏ BAB48352-8	#28	The Cuckoo Clock of Doom	$3.99
❏ BAB48347-1	#29	Monster Blood III	$3.99
❏ BAB48348-X	#30	It Came from Beneath the Sink	$3.99
❏ BAB48349-8	#31	The Night of the Living Dummy II	$3.99
❏ BAB48344-7	#32	The Barking Ghost	$3.99
❏ BAB48345-5	#33	The Horror at Camp Jellyjam	$3.99
❏ BAB48346-3	#34	Revenge of the Lawn Gnomes	$3.99
❏ BAB48340-4	#35	A Shocker on Shock Street	$3.99
❏ BAB56873-6	#36	The Haunted Mask II	$3.99
❏ BAB56874-4	#37	The Headless Ghost	$3.99
❏ BAB56875-2	#38	The Abominable Snowman of Pasadena	$3.99
❏ BAB56876-0	#39	How I Got My Shrunken Head	$3.99
❏ BAB56877-9	#40	Night of the Living Dummy III	$3.99
❏ BAB56878-7	#41	Bad Hare Day	$3.99
❏ BAB56879-5	#42	Egg Monsters from Mars	$3.99
❏ BAB56880-9	#43	The Beast from the East	$3.99
❏ BAB56881-7	#44	Say Cheese and Die–Again!	$3.99
❏ BAB56882-5	#45	Ghost Camp	$3.99
❏ BAB56883-3	#46	How to Kill a Monster	$3.99
❏ BAB56884-1	#47	Legend of the Lost Legend	$3.99
❏ BAB56885-X	#48	Attack of the Jack-O'-Lanterns	$3.99
❏ BAB56886-8	#49	Vampire Breath	$3.99
❏ BAB56887-6	#50	Calling All Creeps	$3.99

GOOSEBUMPS PRESENTS

❏ BAB74586-7	Goosebumps Presents TV Episode #1 The Girl Who Cried Monster	$3.99
❏ BAB74587-5	Goosebumps Presents TV Episode #2 The Cuckoo Clock of Doom	$3.99
❏ BAB74588-3	Goosebumps Presents TV Episode #3 Welcome to Camp Nightmare	$3.99
❏ BAB74589-1	Goosebumps Presents TV Episode #4 Return of the Mummy	$3.99
❏ BAB74590-5	Goosebumps Presents TV Episode #5 Night of the Living Dummy II	$3.99

☐ BAB62836-4	Tales to Give You Goosebumps Book & Light Set Special Edition #1	$11.95
☐ BAB26603-9	More Tales to Give You Goosebumps Book & Light Set Special Edition #2	$11.95
☐ BAB74150-4	Even More Tales to Give You Goosebumps Book and Boxer Shorts Pack Special Edition #3	$14.99

GIVE YOURSELF GOOSEBUMPS

☐ BAB55323-2	Give Yourself Goosebumps #1: Escape from the Carnival of Horrors	$3.99
☐ BAB56645-8	Give Yourself Goosebumps #2: Tick Tock, You're Dead	$3.99
☐ BAB56646-6	Give Yourself Goosebumps #3: Trapped in Bat Wing Hall	$3.99
☐ BAB67318-1	Give Yourself Goosebumps #4: The Deadly Experiments of Dr. Eeek	$3.99
☐ BAB67319-X	Give Yourself Goosebumps #5: Night in Werewolf Woods	$3.99
☐ BAB67320-3	Give Yourself Goosebumps #6: Beware of the Purple Peanut Butter	$3.99
☐ BAB67321-1	Give Yourself Goosebumps #7: Under the Magician's Spell	$3.99
☐ BAB84765-1	Give Yourself Goosebumps #8: The Curse of the Creeping Coffin	$3.99
☐ BAB84766-X	Give Yourself Goosebumps #9: The Knight in Screaming Armor	$3.99
☐ BAB84767-8	Give Yourself Goosebumps #10: Diary of a Mad Mummy	$3.99
☐ BAB84768-6	Give Yourself Goosebumps #11: Deep in the Jungle of Doom	$3.99
☐ BAB84772-4	Give Yourself Goosebumps #12: Welcome to the Wicked Wax Museum	$3.99

☐ BAB53770-9	The Goosebumps Monster Blood Pack	$11.95
☐ BAB50995-0	The Goosebumps Monster Edition #1	$12.95
☐ BAB93371-X	The Goosebumps Monster Edition #2	$12.95
☐ BAB60265-9	Goosebumps Official Collector's Caps Collecting Kit	$5.99
☐ BAB73906-9	Goosebumps Postcard Book	$7.95

Scare me, thrill me, mail me GOOSEBUMPS now!

Available wherever you buy books, or use this order form. Scholastic Inc., P.O. Box 7502,
2931 East McCarty Street, Jefferson City, MO 65102

Please send me the books I have checked above. I am enclosing $_____ (please add $2.00 to cover shipping and handling). Send check or money order — no cash or C.O.D.s please.

Name _____ Age _____

Address _____

City _____ State/Zip_____

Please allow four to six weeks for delivery. Offer good in the U.S. only. Sorry, mail orders are not available to residents of Canada. Prices subject to change.

GB5962